THE Sisters 8

BOOK 8

ZINNIA'S ZANINESS

By Lauren Baratz-Logsted
With Greg Logsted and Jackie Logsted

sandpiper

HOUGHTON MIFFLIN HARCOURT

BOSTON • NEW YORK • 2011

SANDPIPER and the SAND[] logo are trademarks of Houghton Mifflin Harcourt Publishing Company.

www.hmhbooks.com

The text of this book is set in Youbee. Book design by Carol Chu.

Library of Congress Cataloging-in-Publication Data
Baratz-Logsted, Lauren.
Zinnia's zaniness / by Lauren Baratz-Logsted with Greg Logsted and Jackie Logsted.
p. cm.—(The sisters eight ; bk. 8) Summary: With the arrival of August, Zinnia, the youngest of the Huit octuplets, eagerly anticipates getting her power and gift, both of which hold big surprises that are revealed to the sisters on their eighth birthday. [1. Abandoned children—Fiction. 2. Sisters—Fiction. 3. Vacations—Fiction. 4. Birthdays—Fiction. 5. Humorous stories.] I. Logsted, Greg. II. Logsted, Jackie. III. Title.
PZ7.B22966Zin 2011[Fic]—dc22
2010039257

ISBN 978-0-547-55438-9 paper over board
ISBN 978-0-547-55439-6 paperback

Manufactured in the United States of America • DOC 10 9 8 7 6 5 4 3 2 •
4500326251

For Emma Fagan,
a mighty friend.

Annie   Durinda   Georgia   Jackie

Marcia   Petal   Rebecca   Zinnia

PROLOGUE

Clean my fingernails or don't clean my fingernails? Clean my fingernails or don't clean my fingernails? Clean my—

Oh, hello!

You really are still here, aren't you? It's good to see you, I suppose. And I further suppose you think it's good to see me.

Me.

Me, me, me.

Mi-mi-mi-mi-mi!

Oops, sorry. I just lapsed into song for a moment there, practicing my opera singing. But we weren't talking about *mi,* were we? We were talking about me.

Me.

Now, there's something that's been occupying your mind, hasn't it—the subject of who *I* am. In fact, it's been occupying your mind ever since you first heard about the Sisters Eight, which of course you first heard about from *me.*

You wonder: *Who is that person who keeps talking to us in the prologues?* You wonder: *Are we supposed to* know that voice from somewhere? You wonder: *And does it matter?*

One thing's for certain: I have to be Someone. I mean, I can't be No One, can I? If I were No One, I'd certainly be the most Chatty Cathy of a No One ever.

I'm here to tell you, I'm definitely Someone. In fact — hold on to your hats! — you have already met me in the Sisters Eight books. Well, maybe not *me* in person, as in seeing my face and my body, but you have met my syntax.

Ring any bells yet?

Now, if Jackie were by my side right now, she'd explain that syntax has to do with the way words are put together. So you could say that my personal syntax, not to mention my overall tone, is like a set of fingerprints that give me away. Lots of people have fingers, but no two sets of fingerprints are exactly alike. You can catch a criminal by his or her fingerprints. You'd do well to keep that in mind.

Still not ringing any bells?

Fine. I'll give you one hint:

Dear Rebecca,

I always knew you were a fiery girl — nice work!

And:

> I must say, with you involved, it was always touch and go if this day would ever arrive.

Okay, so maybe that's two hints. So sue me.

Now do you have it? I certainly hope you do. I could give you tons of other examples — well, maybe not tons, but at least a dozen — but honestly, if you haven't figured it out by now . . .

I'm the being the Eights keep referring to as the note leaver.

That's right. Those notes left behind the loose stone in the wall of the drawing room? My handiwork. Mine, all mine. Me.

I suppose now that you know I'm the note leaver, you'd like to know my name too. Isn't that just like people? Give them an inch, they want it all.

Well, we don't have time for that right now because Zinnia's been waiting to have her turn quite long enough. It would be cruel to keep her waiting any longer.

Before I turn the story over to the story, though, I suppose I do need to remind you of the Eights' individual powers and gifts, just in case you've forgotten since last we met.

Annie: power — can think like an adult when necessary; gift — purple ring

Durinda: power — can freeze people, except Zinnia; gift — green earrings

Georgia: power — can become invisible; gift — gold compact

Jackie: power — faster than a speeding train; gift — red cape

Marcia: power — x-ray vision; gift — purple cloak

Petal: power — can read people's minds; gift — silver charm bracelet

Rebecca: power — can shoot fire from her fingertips; gift — a locket

I wonder what Zinnia's power and gift will be. I wonder if either will prove to be as much of a doozy as Zinnia has been hoping for. I rather hope so. I have a certain soft spot for Zinnia.

But there's no time to wonder about that or anything else now because it really is . . .

Zinnia time.

ONE

"Why so glum, chums?" asked Pete.

It was Friday morning, August 1, and we were all hanging around in the drawing room, doing nothing but slouching where we sat, except for Georgia, who was lying on her back on the floor, throwing a ball toward the ceiling and catching it, over and over again. Even the cats were slouching, except for Greatorex, who kept leaping upward in hopes of catching Georgia's ball.

Pete had entered a moment ago with Mrs. Pete. Mrs. Pete had her hair up in curlers while Pete was dressed in his work uniform of a navy blue T-shirt and dangerously low-slung jeans. He had his tool belt on.

We liked Pete's tool belt.

"We are not glum," Annie corrected him. "We are depressed."

"With good cause," Durinda added.

"Okay," Pete said. "Why are you depressed, then?"

"Because it is August," Georgia said, throwing her ball at the ceiling again.

"I don't understand," Pete said. "Isn't that a good thing? August means no more chance of Rebecca shooting fire from her fingertips and perhaps accidentally burning the house down around our ears."

"There is that," Jackie said in an attempt at optimism. But even she couldn't keep that up for very long. She sighed and added, "August seems so very long this year. A whole thirty-one days."

"But that's good, isn't it?" Pete tried again. "You have a whole month of summer vacation left before you go back to school."

"Our birthday is this month," Marcia said. "On August eighth, beginning at eight a.m., we will begin turning eight at the rate of one Eight per minute."

"I did remember that," Pete said. "But isn't *that* a good thing?"

We had to give Pete credit: he did keep trying.

"It is not," Petal said. "For the first time in our lives, Mommy and Daddy will not be with us on our birthday." A tear escaped Petal's eye then, but for once none of us moved to comfort her, not even Durinda or Jackie, because tears were beginning to escape all of our eyes.

"I see," Pete said softly.

"I miss having the ability to shoot fire from my fingertips," Rebecca said. "I know I made a promise not to use that power anymore unless necessary, but I miss just the very idea of that power."

"I thought I would be happy for it to be August," Zinnia said. "It being August means that it is my turn, finally, to get my power and my gift."

"Okay, now I'm sure *that's* a good thing." Pete tried yet again.

We were still willing to give him credit for persistence, but we did think it was time he got a clue gun. He needed to just give up. Couldn't he see that we would not be cheered? That we *could* not be cheered?

"I will be the eighth Eight to get my power and gift," Zinnia said, "after which, according to that first note we found behind the loose stone, we will finally discover what happened to Mommy and Daddy when they disappeared."

"Or died," Rebecca added.

Yes, Rebecca was back to that again. Well, who could blame her for being in a dark mood? We were all in dark moods.

"Now, I know you will try to say that is a good thing, Mr. Pete," Petal said.

We looked at Pete standing there opening his mouth to speak, and we saw that Petal had been right: of course he was about to say that.

"Well, not a good thing if we're talking about what

Rebecca said," Marcia corrected Petal. "Rather, you'll say that what Zinnia said is a good thing."

"The part about finding out what happened to Mommy and Daddy," Jackie said, just so we were all clear. "That's what you'll say is a good thing."

"The problem is," Georgia said, "we are at August first now but August is a whole thirty-one days. Oh, why couldn't August be a shorter month, like June or September? Really, the best thing would be if August were like February, only not during a leap year."

"Georgia's right," Durinda said. Things had to be pretty bad around here if Durinda was agreeing with Georgia. "I think I could bear to wait twenty-eight days to finally learn the truth," Durinda went on. "But waiting thirty-one whole days is really just too much. Then, too, there's always the question *What if the answer is something truly awful?* What will we do then?"

"We usually take a vacation in the summer," Annie said, bringing the conversational ball full circle. We'd begun with Annie and gone one by one down to Zinnia, then back up to Annie again. Sometimes we felt as though our talking was like other people practicing musical scales. "We usually take one in the winter over the holidays and another in the summer. But this summer there won't be one, not without Mommy and Daddy here."

"But what about the trip we took to France?" Pete said.

"That doesn't count as a real vacation," Annie said. "We went there for a wedding, so it was more like a working holiday."

"You could still take a real vacation," a female voice said.

It took us a while to realize who that voice belonged to. We looked around at one another. Nope, that wasn't any of our voices. And it certainly wasn't Pete's. Then we realized it was Mrs. Pete. Pete had been hogging the conversation ball so much, we'd forgotten she was even in the room!

And because it took us a moment to identify the speaker and then another moment to get over our shock at who was actually speaking, it took a further moment for what she'd said to fully register.

"But we can't do that," Georgia objected.

"Of course we can't," Durinda said, once again, shockingly, agreeing with Georgia.

"We can go by ourselves to do a Big Shop," Marcia said.

"Or even a Really Big Shop if necessary," Jackie said.

"But we can't go on a whole vacation all by ourselves," Annie said.

"It is tempting, though," Rebecca said.

"Eight little girls on vacation all by themselves?" Zinnia said. "That would draw too much attention."

"Drawing attention is always a bad thing," Petal

said. "Draw attention to yourself and before you know it, your jig is up. Nope. Sorry. No can do. Perhaps another year. Or better yet, never."

"I meant that we could take you on a vacation," Mrs. Pete said gently.

"We could!" Pete said, taking the conversational ball back from Mrs. Pete. Huh. We'd never noticed before how much more of the talking he did. Maybe it was a guy thing?

Georgia made a face at him. "But don't you have to work for a living?"

"I have read about that," Marcia said. "If a person is supposed to work for a living and he stops doing it for too long, it can be a really bad thing."

"We'd hate to see Bill Collector come after you, Mr. Pete," Petal said solemnly.

Poor Petal. She still believed that all bill collectors were called Bill Collector, even though the only person we'd ever met who was actually named Bill Collector had been very nice to us and hadn't taken any of our money at all.

"I am allowed to take a vacation from time to time," Pete said.

"Seems to me that all you ever do lately," Rebecca said, "is take time off from work."

"I don't think this is really the moment for that, Rebecca," Jackie pointed out. "When the Petes are kind enough to offer to take us on vacation, it hardly seems appropriate to point out Mr. Pete's recent lax work habits."

"I want to go on a vacation!" Zinnia said.

"Oh, I don't know about this," Petal said worriedly. "Don't vacations sometimes end badly for people? If we stay home, we need never find out the answer to that question."

We ignored Petal.

"But if we did go," Annie said, "*where* would we go?"

"Yes," Georgia said, "where? After all, we've already been to Utah, the Big City, and France. What's left?"

The Petes thought about this for a long moment. Well, who could blame them for needing time? It was a tough question. What *was* left?

"The Seaside!" Pete burst out excitedly.

"Oh, I've always wanted to go," Mrs. Pete said.

The Seaside.

Oh, that did sound heavenly.

Suddenly, despite how glum we'd been earlier, we could feel ourselves growing excited. We were daring to hope, daring to dream.

"How would we get there?" Annie asked.

That was Annie all over, we thought, always insisting on being practical.

"I'd suggest my flatbed pickup," Pete said, "but you might get wet if it rains, plus there are no seat belts back there, which is too unsafe for a long road trip, so we'll take your Hummer."

"Thank the universe," Petal said, heaving a little sigh of relief, "that at least *someone* is thinking of safety issues. And thank the universe that we won't be traveling by train or plane. I've had quite enough of those modes of transportation for the time being, thank you very much."

"When would we leave?" Annie said, still being practical.

"Tomorrow," Pete said decisively. "That'll give us today to pack and shop for anything we might need."

"Shopping," Annie mused, "that's good. There are some things I think we should bring with us."

"You mean like sunscreen?" Petal said. "And sunscreen with SPF one hundred for me so that I do not burn to a crisp from the Seaside sun's strong rays?"

"That too," Annie said with a disturbing air of mystery.

What *could* she be thinking of? we wondered.

"And how long will we be gone for?" Annie said, *still* being practical.

"We'll return on August ninth," Pete said, still decisively. "That way we'll be gone from Saturday to Saturday, a good length for any vacation, plus we'll be away from home for your birthday, so you won't have the sadness of celebrating your birthday here without your parents."

This sounded like a good idea to us. If we were somewhere else on our birthday, we wouldn't be constantly looking around the house and envisioning scenes of birthdays past when our parents had been with us. Still, just thinking of spending our birthday *anywhere* without our parents made us sad, so we took a moment to bow our heads.

"So," Pete said, after he'd given us sufficient time for our moment of sadness, "is everyone in agreement? Because we can't go if anyone objects."

"I agree!" Annie said.

"I agree!" Georgia said.

"I agree!" Jackie said.

"I agree!" Marcia said.

"I agree!" Petal said. Then she added, "But with grave reservations."

"I agree!" Rebecca said.

"I *definitely* agree!" Zinnia said.

Mrs. Pete turned to the one non-agreeing Eight. "Durinda?"

"Just who exactly is going to be doing all the cooking on this so-called vacation?" Durinda asked suspiciously.

"We'll go out to eat a lot, I suspect," Pete said. "And if we stay someplace where we have our own kitchen and want to eat in from time to time . . . ?"

"I'll help you, Durinda," Jackie offered.

"We all will," six other Eights also offered.

"That sounds like too many cooks in my kitchen," Durinda said. "Still, I suppose I agree too."

"Yippee!" Zinnia said. "We're going on vacation!"

"But are you really sure you can take so much time off from work?" Rebecca asked Pete. "Won't your boss have some sort of objection?"

Oh, Rebecca.

"I *am* my boss!" Pete was upset. "Why do you think it's called Pete's Repairs and Auto Wrecking? So I think it's safe to say I can give myself the time off without firing me. As for all the cars in the area, they'll just have to refrain from breaking down or needing wrecking while I'm gone."

"Yippee!" Zinnia said. "We're going on vacation!"

"Why don't you all start packing," Annie suggested, "while I go put on my Daddy disguise so I can go shopping and pick up everything we need."

"What about the cats?" Zinnia asked Pete.

Zinnia was referring to Anthrax, Dandruff, Greatorex, Jaguar, Minx, Precious, Rambunctious, and Zither, our eight gray and white puffball cats, one cat per Eight. There was also Old Felix, the Petes' cat, who'd been living with us ever since the Petes temporarily moved in.

"Why, they'll come with us," Pete said. "We can't leave them home alone for a week. I'm sure we can find somewhere to stay that will be happy to have all of us and the cats too."

We weren't sure he should be so sure about that, but we didn't say anything, not wanting to rock the vacation boat.

"Yippee!" Zinnia said. "The cats are going on vacation too!"

We no longer felt glum at all, not even a bit. In fact, as we all hurried to the door so we could begin doing all we needed to do before going away, we were feeling very excited indeed.

"Wait a second," Marcia said, for some reason turning around. "What's that loose stone doing shoving itself a little ways out from the wall?"

We turned.

It was true. The loose stone was jutting out a bit. This, in our experience, could mean only one thing: a new note.

"But that makes no sense," Marcia said. "There should only be a new note if Zinnia has received her power or her gift, neither of which has happened yet."

Marcia crossed the room and angrily pushed the loose stone back into place.

Marcia had had issues with the note leaver ever since Rebecca's month, when we'd discovered Rebecca had superhuman strength but a note to accompany that

never came. Marcia went back and forth now between concern over the note leaver and anger at the note leaver.

"Silly note leaver," Marcia muttered, following the rest of us out of the room.

If she had turned then, if any of us had turned, we would have seen something that we could only have taken as ominous:

The loose stone had already popped itself back out again, as though it were trying to tell us something.

Good thing we didn't turn.

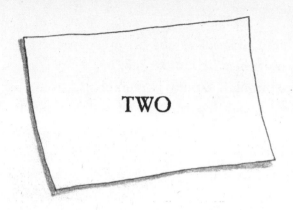

TWO

The next morning found us in our bedrooms putting the finishing touches on our packing.

In bedroom 2, Zinnia looked from Rebecca to Petal to Durinda.

"Rebecca," Zinnia asked, "why are you wearing your locket?"

"Because I always do." Rebecca shrugged. "What's it to you?"

"Petal," Zinnia asked, "why are you wearing your charm bracelet?"

"Because I haven't taken it off since receiving it, not even when I bathe?" Petal asked-answered, as though worried. "Is that the right response?"

"Durinda," Zinnia said, "why are you wearing your dangly earrings with the green stones? And *don't* say because you always do. I know that's not true. They're so fancy, you hardly ever wear them."

"I don't know the right answer," Durinda said,

sounding like Petal as she fingered an earring. "I'll let you know when I think of one."

"Harrumph," Zinnia harrumphed, stomping out of bedroom 2, passing through the connecting bathroom, and opening the door to bedroom 1 with Durinda, Petal, and Rebecca close on her heels.

"Annie, Georgia, Jackie, Marcia," Zinnia said accusingly, her hand on the doorknob, "just what do you think you are doing?"

"What?" Annie, Georgia, Jackie, and Marcia said, looking guilty.

"Annie, you're wearing your purple ring," Zinnia accused. "Georgia, don't bother trying to hide that compact in your hand because I can see the gold glittering between your fingers. Jackie, is there a good reason to pack your red cape for a trip to the Seaside in August?

Marcia, same question for you, only substitute *purple cloak* for *red cape*."

"We're sorry," Jackie said. "Petal thought it wouldn't be safe for us to leave our gifts behind."

"And for once," Georgia said, "we thought the little idiot might be right about something."

"Oh, fine, blame me," Petal said. "Now Zinnia will probably hate me forever and that shall be very bad since Zinnia has always been the kindest to me. Well, except for maybe Durinda. And of course Jackie."

We could tell Annie was a little miffed at being left off Petal's List of Kind People but we were too busy worrying about Zinnia to worry about Annie.

"Didn't it occur to anyone that I might be offended," Zinnia said, "that I might feel *hurt,* since I'm the only Eight without a gift to bring with me on vacation?"

"We're sorry," Durinda said, putting her arm around Zinnia.

"We didn't mean to hurt you," Jackie added, putting her arm around Zinnia from the other side.

"I know!" Annie suggested excitedly in what some of us felt was a thinly disguised attempt to prove she could be as kind as the next Eight. "Why don't you pick something from the house to bring with you — you know, something you personally consider special — so that special something can be your stand-in gift while we're away?"

"Can it be anything?" Zinnia asked.

"Anything," Annie assured her.

A grin as wide as a cape or a cloak spread straight across Zinnia's face.

* * * * * * * *

"Oh no, you are not," Rebecca said, charging down the stairs after Zinnia.

Well, we were all charging at that point.

"Oh yes, I am!" Zinnia shouted gleefully back at us. "Annie said I could bring anything!"

"But I didn't say you could bring *two* anythings!" Annie shouted forward at Zinnia.

"Even I know that if we bring those two . . . *things*," Petal added, "other people will think we are odd."

"And do we really need any more of that in our lives?" Georgia said.

Zinnia reached the bottom of the stairs, which we admit was a very long flight, and headed toward the drawing room, seven Eights in hot pursuit.

That was when Pete blew a whistle.

Oh no. Pete had a whistle. We certainly hoped he didn't plan on blowing it at us a lot while on vacation. That could get annoying.

"Hang on," Pete said, holding one palm up traffic-cop style and causing us to skid to a stop, crashing into each other one by one. "Now, what's all the fuss here?"

Eight Eights spoke at once, so it took a moment for him to sort out what we were saying, but eventually he seemed to get the idea.

"Let me see if I've got this straight," Pete said as

Mrs. Pete came over to join him. "Seven of you are bringing your special gifts on vacation because you're worried they'll get stolen if you leave them home. Zinnia's upset because she doesn't have a special gift to bring. Annie said she could take along whatever she wanted from the house to be her stand-in gift until the real thing comes along. Zinnia wants to bring that suit of armor and dressmaker's dummy that you lot refer to as Daddy Sparky and Mommy Sally."

It was true, we had to admit with embarrassment. Zinnia *did* want to take the suit of armor and the dressmaker's dummy on vacation with us. Could she *be* any zanier?

"And now," Pete said in conclusion, "Petal, of all people — sorry, Petal, but I think you understand — *Petal,* the same Petal who hid under beds in not one but two different countries for the better part of the month of June, is concerned that other people might think you lot are odd?"

Eight heads nodded.

"I'm sorry to have to be the one to tell you this," Pete said, "but that ship has already sailed."

"He means that everyone already thinks we're odd," Jackie said.

"There was no need to translate, Jackie," Annie said. "We were all able to figure out that figure of speech on our own."

"I wasn't," Petal said.

"Does this mean that it's okay with you, Mr. Pete," Zinnia asked, "if Daddy Sparky and Mommy Sally come along for the ride?"

"I don't see why not," Pete said.

"Phew," Zinnia said.

Even though we'd never have admitted it out loud, we shared Zinnia's *phew.* The Petes were great, but since New Year's Eve, we'd grown kind of used to having Daddy Sparky and Mommy Sally as our stand-in parents. They may not have been big talkers, and their versions of hugs did leave something to be desired, but we had missed them when we went to France — you simply can't take a suit of armor on an airplane with you, what with all those metal detectors, plus we couldn't possibly split up Daddy Sparky and Mommy Sally — and we would have missed them if we had to leave them a second time.

"But if Daddy Sparky and Mommy Sally are with us," Petal worried aloud, "and we're all gone too, plus the cats, who will keep an eye on the house? You can't leave a house behind with no one to keep an eye on it. It's unsafe!"

"People usually ask their neighbors to keep an eye out," Durinda said.

"Somehow," Annie said, "I don't think asking the Wicket to do that is such a good idea."

Did we really need her to tell us that?

"What about Carl the talking refrigerator and robot Betty?" Pete suggested.

"Haven't you noticed," Georgia said, "that Carl's a talking refrigerator but not a walking refrigerator? If someone bad breaks in, what can he do? Toss ice cubes at them? He certainly can't chase them anywhere."

"Haven't you noticed," Rebecca added, "that robot Betty never follows instructions? Tell her to keep all the riffraff out, you know she'll just go watch TV."

"Since Carl the talking refrigerator and robot Betty won't do us any good if we leave them behind," Petal said, "can we take them with us this time?"

We ignored Petal.

"I'm sure everything will be just fine here," Pete said.

"Can we go get Daddy Sparky and Mommy Sally from the drawing room," Zinnia asked, "so we can begin loading them and everything else into the car?"

Zinnia didn't wait for an answer.

And as the rest of us followed her into the drawing room, we saw that the loose stone was once again sticking out.

"Silly note leaver," Marcia muttered, shoving the stone back in again.

"Stop doing that," Zinnia said, upset. "It's my month.

I should be in charge of shoving the loose stone back in if it needs it."

Just as Zinnia finished her last sentence, the stone popped out again.

Marcia reached to shove it back in but Zinnia stopped her just in time.

"I *said*," Zinnia said with rare forcefulness, "that's *my* job this month."

Then Zinnia reached for the stone, but instead of shoving it back in again, she slid it the rest of the way out.

"Well, what do you know?" Zinnia said, peering into the space where the stone had been. "There *is* a note back here."

We all gathered round as Zinnia pulled out the note and began to read:

Dear Zinnia,

It seems I've been waiting to say this to you for far too long: Congratulations on your magnificent power!

Of course, I did try to congratulate you yesterday, at the earliest possible moment of your official month, but <u>someone</u> shoved the stone back in. So I was forced to congratulate you today instead.

Fifteen down, one to go. I do hope you've been enjoying your power. I hope you agree that it is, as you would say, a doozy!

As always, the note was unsigned.

We did think that it would be nice if, just once, the note leaver forgot about not signing his or her — or its — name, and went ahead and signed it. Who could this person be?

"I don't understand this," Marcia said, frustrated.

"This is ridiculous," Rebecca said. "Zinnia hasn't received any power."

"Maybe I have," Zinnia said in a small voice.

"That's crazy talk," Georgia said. "Can you think like an adult?"

"I don't know how I'd know if I could do that," Zinnia said, "but I'm fairly certain I can't."

"Can you make other people freeze?" Annie asked.

Zinnia tried rapidly hitting her palm against her leg and then pointing at various ones of us but none of us froze.

"No," Zinnia said, "nor can anyone freeze me."

"Can you make yourself disappear?" Durinda asked.

Zinnia twitched her nose twice. "Can you still see me?" she asked hopefully.

"'Fraid so," Durinda said.

"Then I guess the answer must be no," Zinnia said sadly.

"Can you run faster than a speeding train?" Marcia asked.

"Do you have one handy?" Zinnia asked. Then, not waiting for a response, she added, "I'm sure I can't, even if you did."

"Do you have x-ray vision?" Jackie asked.

Zinnia squinched her eyes tight. "No," she said.

"Good," Petal said. "That means you can't see my underwear."

"Can you read people's minds?" Rebecca asked.

"No," Zinnia said, "but I can guess what you're thinking about me and I know it's not good. And before you ask, no, I can't shoot fire from my fingertips."

"Then what *can* you do?" Georgia demanded.

"I can talk to the cats," Zinnia said simply. "I can understand them and they can understand me." She shrugged. "It's the same power I've had all my life."

"That's not a power," Georgia said, laughing in her face. "That's just your insanity."

One day we would regret doing it, but in that moment, we laughed at Zinnia too.

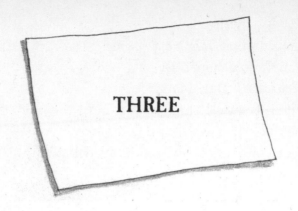

THREE

"Let's pack up the car so we can hit the road!" seven of us cried with great enthusiasm and one of us cried with half enthusiasm. That half enthusiast would be Zinnia, who, we suspected, still felt bad that we'd laughed at her. But we weren't worried. She'd get over it. She always did.

"I've got the packing manifest here," Annie said, pulling out a pen and clipboard to which she'd attached a sheet of paper.

"Must we have a packing manifest?" Georgia groaned.

"Can't we just pack the car without one, like normal people?" Rebecca added.

"I don't even know what a manifest is," Petal said. "Will it hurt, like getting a shot at the doctor's office?"

"No," Jackie reassured her. "A *manifest* in the way Annie's using it is simply a fancy name for a list."

Annie stood beside Mrs. Pete, checking off items on her list as Pete loaded the purple Hummer.

"Ten suitcases?" Annie called to Pete.

"Check!" he called back.

"The big bag we'll take to the beach with items like regular sunscreen for the rest of us and SPF one hundred for Petal?" Annie called.

"Check!" Pete called back.

"Snacks for the ride?" Annie called.

"Check!" Pete called back.

"How long will the ride be?" Petal asked.

We ignored her.

"Our eight cats plus Old Felix and all the cat things?" Annie called.

"Check!" Pete called back.

"Daddy Sparky and Mommy Sally?" Annie called.

"Check!" Pete called back. He sounded like he might be getting tired and out of breath. We hadn't known that could happen to Pete. "Are we almost finished with your manifest, Annie?" he asked. "It's getting a little cramped in there. I'm not sure there will be room for all of us humans if you try to cram any more stuff in."

"That's okay," Annie said, "because there's just one box left."

"A box?" Pete looked surprised, and then he saw Annie point to a box near her feet. "What's in that box?" he wanted to know. "I don't remember seeing the word *box* anywhere on your manifest."

"Oh, it's just something we Eights need to take on

vacation with us," Annie said with that disturbing air of mystery again.

"Oof!" Pete said, lifting the box off the ground. "This box is heavy. What have you got in here, old books?"

"Never mind that now," Annie said as Pete crammed that one last item into the Hummer. "We need to go say goodbye to Carl the talking refrigerator and robot Betty."

* * * * * * * *

Clink, clink, clink.

The ice-cube dispenser was making rapid clinking noises, which in our house could mean only one thing: the talking refrigerator was crying.

"Stop crying, Carl," Durinda said. "We'll come back."

"Don't forget to eat proper meals while you're away from me," Carl the talking refrigerator said morosely.

Clink, clink.

"We won't," Durinda assured him, spreading her arms wide to give him a hug.

"Just because it's summer," Carl said, "doesn't mean you can eat ice cream all day long."

"We know that, Carl," Durinda said.

"But I *will* keep the ice cream at home perfectly chilled for your return," Carl said.

Clink.

"We know that too, Carl," Durinda said. "You always take such good care of us."

"Durinda," Rebecca said, "do you think you could stop hugging the talking refrigerator already so we could leave on our vacation?"

"Oops, sorry," Durinda said with a blush as she forced herself away from Carl. "I hadn't realized I was still doing that."

"Goodbye, Carl!" we all shouted as we headed for the door.

"Goodbye, Betty!" we all shouted as we passed her on our way out the door. "Take good care of Carl for us!"

The robot slammed the door behind us.

It was anyone's guess what the robot would do with us gone.

But at that moment, all we were thinking was *Yippee! Vacation time!*

* * * * * * * *

"One hundred boxes of juice on the wall, one hundred boxes of juice! You take one down, pass it around, ninety-nine boxes of juice on the wall!"

Big breath.

"Ninety-nine boxes of juice on the wall, ninety-nine bo—"

"Excuse me," Pete said, interrupting our singing, which we'd decided to take random turns at so that no one's voice gave out before the end of the song, "but why do you say 'boxes of juice'?"

"What else would we say?" Jackie asked.

"Well," Marcia said, "I believe in the original song, it's 'bottles of beer.'"

"We can't sing about bottles of beer," Petal said. "We're kids. We could get arrested for that."

"That's not what I meant," Pete said.

"Then why don't you say what you meant so that we'll all know?" Rebecca said.

Oh, Rebecca.

Near the end of July we'd grown hopeful about Rebecca. She'd seemed so much more mature, nicer even.

But that hadn't lasted. That had been our experience with most people: they changed very little or, if they did change a lot, they soon went back to the way they'd been before the changing. Now Rebecca was pretty much back to being Rebecca, which meant awful. Oh, well. At least she wasn't using her superhuman strength to do any of us grievous bodily harm. We figured we would take what we could get.

"It's just that I happen to know that your favorite flavor of juice is mango," Pete said.

"I prefer just plain glasses of pulp," Rebecca said.

We ignored her.

"So I guess what I was wondering was," Pete said, "why don't you sing 'One hundred boxes of mango juice on the wall, one hundred,' and so on and so forth?"

"Who was doing the singing when we got interrupted?" Georgia said.

"I was," Durinda said. "I was doing ninety-nine."

"Please sing Mr. Pete's version," Annie said, "so he can see."

"Perhaps I'd better start at the beginning," Durinda said. "I seem to have forgotten where I left off."

"Just do it!" Rebecca shouted.

Do you see what we mean about Rebecca?

"Ninety-nine boxes of mango juice on the wall, ninety-nine boxes of mango juice! You take one down, pass it around, ninety-eight boxes of mango juice on the wall!"

"Do you see now, Mr. Pete?" Jackie asked gently.

"No," Pete said. "I see nothing except for the road in front of me. Oops! Train crossing!"

Whoa, that was close.

"Don't even bother, girls," Mrs. Pete said as the train finished crossing our path and we were safe to drive over the railroad tracks. "He's always been like this."

"I've always been like what?" Pete said, sounding offended.

"I hate to say it," Mrs. Pete said, "but you don't really have any rhythm."

"I'm afraid she's right, Mr. Pete," Marcia said. "The two syllables that the word *mango* adds throw off the entire rhythm of the song."

Pete hummed quietly to himself for a time before bursting out with "I do believe you're right — I've got no rhythm!"

* * * * * * * *

"Fifty-three boxes of juice on the wall, fifty-three boxes of juice! You take one down, pass it around, fifty-two boxes of juice on the wall!"

"Nice singing, Zinnia," Annie said. "Who wants to go next?"

"How long have we been driving?" Petal asked.

Judging from the changes in the sky, at least a few hours had passed since we'd left home, but we didn't say that because Petal might worry we'd been driving so long our car would fall off the edge of the Earth.

We hate to admit it, but we were fairly certain there were moments Petal believed the Earth was flat.

"How long until we get there?" Petal asked.

We ignored this question too because we didn't know the answer. Who knew how long it would take us to get where we were going? We certainly hoped we didn't run out of song first.

"Fine," Petal said, and we realized that the realization that we were going to go on ignoring her questions must have sunk in. "I'll do fifty-two. I'm only glad those are boxes of juice and not bottles. With all of them practically falling off the wall like that, what if one fell on my head? I could get crushed! Although I suppose that one hundred boxes of juice, were they all to fall on my head at once, could kill me just as neatly as one well-placed bottle."

"The song isn't about falling objects!" Georgia said, exasperated. "It's just about taking drinkable items off the wall!"

"Well, but they could fall," Petal said, "and if they did, they could be deadly, so—"

"Never mind," Jackie said, cutting Petal off with a gentle pat on the arm. "I'll take fifty-two."

* * * * * * * *

"Twenty-seven boxes of juice on the wall—"

"Oh, this drive is going by so quickly," Zinnia said with breathless wonder as the pretty world zipped past our window. "Whoever invented this song is a genius!"

* * * * * * * *

"One box—"

"We're here!" Pete announced joyfully, pulling up at the Seaside.

"Hey!" Rebecca was outraged. "That was my turn you just cut off!"

We ignored her.

While ignoring Rebecca, we all piled out of the car to stretch our legs after the long trip. We'd left sometime in the morning and now it was nearly dark out: royal purple, midnight blue, and just a single sliver of gold streaking the sky.

How long had we been on the road?

How long had we been singing that song?

"I'll tell you one thing," Mrs. Pete said, "Zinnia's right. Whoever invented that song is a genius. Why, it kept us happily busy the whole trip!"

"Fine for you to say," Pete said. "You've got rhythm."

"Don't worry, Mr. Pete," Jackie said. "You've got plenty of other good qualities."

"Thanks, pet," Pete said.

"I wonder," Marcia said, "if that song is expandable."

We were too tired after all that time in the car to even ask her what she was talking about, and some of us were even too tired to mock her, so we simply stood there, waiting for her to get on with it.

"It took us right up to the last box of juice in the song to arrive at our destination," Marcia said. "But what if our trip had lasted twice as long? What if it had been half as short? Would that one song last us exactly the entire trip, no matter how long or short the trip might be?"

Even Pete, who was usually polite about Marcia's peculiar displays of her peculiar brand of intelligence, saw fit to ignore that.

"I'll just go see," Pete said, eyeing the long array of hotels, motels, and other touristy-looking places that lined the Seaside, "about getting lodging for us all for the night."

One place that would take all of us? He'd said something about this earlier. We hadn't commented at the time, and we certainly weren't about to comment now, except perhaps to say to ourselves, very quietly: "Oh, Mr. Pete. What can you possibly be thinking?"

One place fitting all? As if.

As if!

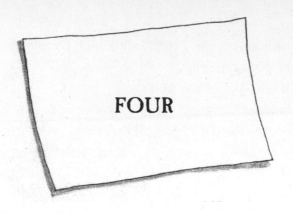

FOUR

"We'll leave all our things in the car while we go find a room," Pete said, "and then we'll come back for them."

Ah, a man with a plan.

"Don't you mean three rooms, Mr. Pete?" Marcia asked him.

"A fourth room for the cats would be nice," Zinnia added. "We don't mind being split up into four and four, but the cats rather prefer to stay all together."

All of us ignored Marcia and Zinnia, including Pete, who probably hadn't planned on springing for an extra room for the week just for the cats.

We set off walking along the boardwalk, looking for a place where we might like to stay. Other people were walking along the boardwalk too, whole families looking happy together. The night air was filled with the sounds of laughter and the smell of cotton candy, and it was all very exciting.

"'The Big Hotel.'" Pete read the large neon sign at the place where we'd stopped. "This looks promising, since we're such a big group."

We strolled into the lobby, which was very big indeed, and then strolled all the way up to the registration desk.

"Welcome to the Big Hotel," the man behind the desk said. "How may I help you?"

"Do you have any rooms available?" Pete asked.

"We do indeed," the man said. "How many will you need?"

"Three," Pete said.

"Four," Zinnia corrected him. "I thought we agreed about the cats."

"I really do think three will be sufficient," Pete said.

"Back up a minute," the man said. "Did you say *cats?*"

Before we could answer, the man stretched across the desk and looked down. He caught sight of eight girls and nine cats, and shock filled his eyes. How had he not noticed us before? we wondered. The man straightened up again.

"I'm sorry, sir," the man said abruptly to Pete, "but there's been a mistake. There are no rooms available here. Please try another hotel."

Pete looked surprised at this sudden turn of events. We suspected he was the only one who was. Not only did Mrs. Pete have all the rhythm, she also had more than her share of common sense.

"I see," Pete said to the man, even though, clearly, he didn't. "Where do you suggest I try?"

The man pointed his finger toward the door that would take us back out to the boardwalk and then hooked his finger to the left. "Try thataway," he said.

"Who says *thataway*?" Rebecca muttered as we headed toward the door. "Where does he think he is, in the middle of a Western?"

Back outside into the boardwalk-strolling throngs, we headed thataway, trying each hotel we came to, all with the same result.

"How about this?" Pete suggested. "The Medium Hotel."

"I wonder if the name refers to the hotel's size," Jackie said, "or that it specifically caters to people who think they can talk to the dead."

"I don't think I want to stay here," Petal said. "It sounds too scary."

We ignored Petal.

And the lady behind the registration desk ignored us when she saw how big a group we were.

"Huh," Pete said, confused as we exited yet another hotel. "I guess people around here don't need our business. You'd think any hotel would be happy to have us."

No, Mr. Pete, we thought, *only* you *would think that.*

The thing was, when our parents were still with us, we'd stayed at hotels from time to time, and we already knew what Pete was only just discovering: no one was ever *happy* to have us.

Back on the boardwalk, Pete looked left and right dejectedly. "Which way now?" he asked.

"How about thataway?" Rebecca said.

So we went thataway and we kept on going thataway until we came to . . .

"The Little Hotel," Pete said. "Look at this puny place, all rundown. Surely it could use our business."

Surely it could not.

The man behind the little registration desk didn't even wait for Pete to ask if there were any rooms available. He simply laughed in our faces.

"I take it the answer is no?" Pete said to the man, who just kept on laughing. "Is it because of the cats?" Pete persisted.

"That too," the man said, looking at us Eights and laughing some more.

Since when were we something to be laughed at? We must say, we were very offended.

"Maybe," Georgia said, "instead of trying places that cater to people who think they can talk to the dead or places that don't seem to want to make any money off us, we should look for a place that caters to people who think they can talk to cats. That way Zinnia could get us in."

The man studied Zinnia with new interest. "Could you talk to my cat?" the man asked. "Orange hasn't been eating lately and I'm worried she might be sick."

Orange. Seven of us laughed. What a silly name for a cat.

"I can try," Zinnia said, ignoring us. "But you mustn't expect too much. If Orange is just meeting me, she might be shy about confessing her deepest, darkest secrets."

The man brought out Orange, who was black, which we agreed made absolutely no sense at all, and set her on the registration desk.

"Can you give me a boost up, Mr. Pete?" Zinnia asked.

Sometimes we forgot how small Zinnia was. In addition to each of us being born a minute apart, with Annie the oldest, each of us was an inch shorter than the previous sister, with Annie the tallest. This meant that Zinnia was a full seven inches shorter than Annie, making Zinnia very short indeed.

Pete did the boosting, and Zinnia and Orange commenced their Eight-to-cat conversation. There was a lot of Zinnia whispering in Orange's furry ear and then Orange doing something that looked like whispering in Zinnia's nonfurry ear.

Occasionally, like now, we were impressed with

Zinnia. What a show she was capable of putting on! A person might almost believe she *could* talk with cats!

Of course, Rebecca would have us change that: *a crazy* person might almost believe that.

Zinnia wrapped up her end of the whispering and told Pete he could stop boosting her. Then she looked up at the man.

"Orange says she is sick," Zinnia said, hurrying to add, "but only in that she is sick of the brand of kibble you've been feeding her. Orange says she wishes you would buy Kitten Kaboodle, the brand with the picture of happy cats on the bag that they're always advertising during the late-late-late movie on channel three-twelve. Orange says the other cats on the boardwalk say it's the best, much better than that cheap Kibble Kan't you've been feeding her."

The man looked embarrassed. "I wasn't meaning to be cheap," he said. "I always thought the cats on the Kibble Kan't bags looked happy enough."

"Not as happy as the Kitten Kaboodle cats," Zinnia insisted. She turned to Jackie. "Jackie, could you run to the car and get the bag of kibble we brought to feed the cats?"

Jackie got the keys from Pete and took off running.

"Jackie's the fastest among us," Durinda explained to the man.

And Jackie proved it, returning very rapidly with the large bag of kibble.

"Do you see now?" Zinnia said to the man as she pointed to the cats on the bag.

The man saw. We all saw.

Zinnia was right: those were some *insanely* happy cats.

"Do you have Orange's kibble bowl handy?" Zinnia asked the man.

"Since she's so fast," the man said, "can I send— what was her name? Jackie?—to go fetch it?"

We just stared at him. How would Jackie know where he kept his cat's kibble bowl?

"I was kidding," he finally said. "Back in a tick."

It was more like a tick *and* a tock—he was no Jackie, after all—but soon he was back with the requested bowl into which Zinnia poured a large serving of Kitten Kaboodle.

Our eight cats plus Old Felix looked at Zinnia like she was crazy to give so much of the good stuff away.

"Don't worry," Zinnia assured them. "There's plenty for everybody."

Orange devoured the Kitten Kaboodle so fast, she was licking her chops in no time.

"As you can see," Zinnia told the man, "Orange is *not* sick."

"She just didn't like the lousy cheap food you were giving her," Georgia added.

"Now that Zinnia has solved your cat problem," Mrs. Pete said, "do you think you might be able to find rooms for us?"

We laughed at the idea of Zinnia solving the man's cat problem. Of course Zinnia hadn't had a conversation with Orange. That whole thing with Kitten Kaboodle was just a lucky guess!

Some of us were getting tired, however. So if Zinnia's lucky guess could get us a room, or three, or four . . .

But the man just laughed in our faces again.

How offensive! And after what Zinnia had done for him. Still, as we watched Rebecca, who'd grown bored and was now playing one-person catch in the tiny lobby using Petal as a human ball, we couldn't say that we blamed him. We were a lot to handle.

But something in our expressions as we turned away from the desk must have caused him to take pity on us.

"Wait," he said. "You still can't stay here, and I can't think of any self-respecting establishment that would have you. But there's a house you might be able to rent for the week."

"A house, you say?" Pete's expression was happy again as we turned to face the man.

"We don't want a house," Georgia said. "We already live in one of those. This is vacation. We want to stay somewhere special."

Oh, Georgia.

"That's fine, that's fine," the man said hurriedly. "It's more of a cottage anyway, but there should be room for all of you. It's all the way at the end of the beach. Goes by the name of the Last-Ditch Cottage. I'm sure no one's using it this week. Almost no one ever does."

"Is it haunted?" Petal asked fearfully.

We ignored Petal, but the man didn't.

"No," he said. Then he shrugged. "Last-Ditch just isn't what most people usually have in mind when they go on vacation."

"It sounds perfect for us, then," Pete said.

Poor Pete. He was finally getting the picture. We weren't "most people."

"Who do I talk to about renting it?" Pete asked.

"You mean right now?" the man asked.

"No, he means next year," Rebecca said. She tossed Petal again before adding in exasperation, "Of course he means now."

Rebecca was being rude, we thought, but she did have a point.

"Oh, it's much too late right now," the man said. "I know a man who knows the man who rents it. Come back in the morning and I'll have the key and the paperwork for you."

"And where do you suggest we sleep until morning?" Mrs. Pete wanted to know.

"I don't know." The man shrugged. "Maybe on the beach?"

* * * * * * * *

Okay, so there were no rooms for us at the inns and maybe we were roughing it more than we were accustomed to, but it was rather cozy on the beach at night, nestled into the sand dunes, with what seemed like a million stars twinkling overhead.

"I hope it doesn't rain," Petal said.

"There's not a cloud in the sky," Pete said.

"I hope we don't get hit by a tidal wave," Petal said.

"I'm sure they don't have those here," Mrs. Pete said.

"Oh, look!" Jackie said. "A shooting star!"

We all looked. How dazzling!

"Quick, make wishes, girls," Mrs. Pete said. "That's what you do when you see a shooting star."

We were grateful she was there to tell us that. We'd never seen a shooting star before and so we didn't know what to do with one, other than be dazzled by it.

"I wish we had that box with us now," Annie said. "Too bad we left it in the car."

"I wish for real French potatoes so that someday I can make real French fries," Durinda said.

"I wish for a bed," Georgia said, "because this sand is lumpy."

"I wish for Georgia to stop complaining," Jackie said, "and to just be happy with wherever she is at the moment, for her sake, not ours."

"I wish for even greater math skills than I already possess," Marcia said.

"I wish to not be scared of everything," Petal said, "and not to die."

"I wish I had a can of pink frosting," Rebecca said.

"I wish it were September already," Zinnia said, "because even though that would mean that my month was over with, my moment in the spotlight history, maybe somehow Mommy and Daddy would be back with us again."

We were all silent for a minute, thinking how much better Zinnia's wish was than any of ours.

Then:

"Oh no! Not a shooting star!" Petal shrieked. "You mean the sky is shooting at us?"

Then she buried her head in the sand.

"Maybe we should just do our Waltons routine and then go to sleep?" Annie suggested with a weary sigh.

Our Waltons routine was something we got from an old TV show. At the end of each episode, the members of the large family each randomly called out good nights to one another.

So that's what we did. We spent a half-hour saying our good nights and then we went to sleep.

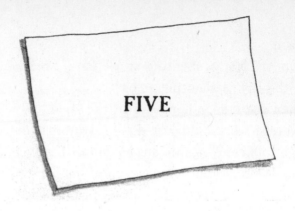

FIVE

The next morning found us up bright and early. We grabbed a quick breakfast on the boardwalk before heading back to the Little Hotel.

"Just sign this paperwork," the man told Pete, "and then I can give you the key."

So Pete did, and the man did, and then we were back in the Hummer, driving all the way to the very end of the beach, where we saw . . .

"I see why it's called the Last-Ditch," Pete said.

"It looks more like a shack than a cottage," Georgia said.

"It's so dingy and gray," Marcia observed.

"It looks like a stiff wind could blow it over," Durinda said.

"Do you think that roof is safe?" Petal worried out loud.

For once we didn't feel that Petal was off base in

being worried. That roof looked like someone had put it on with a cheap stapler.

"I'm sure this will be fine," Pete said as we approached the door, which was at an angle on its hinges.

"Huh," he said as we stepped onto the creaky porch. "It looks like there's a folded piece of paper taped to the door."

"I don't know why there should be a piece of paper there," Annie said. "Didn't you already sign all the paperwork on this place back at the Little Hotel?"

Pete didn't answer. Instead, he untaped the piece of paper and unfolded it.

"Huh," he said again, then he handed the paper to Zinnia. "It's for you."

Zinnia read the note out loud.

Dear Zinnia,

Have I said it yet today? Congratulations on your doozy of a power!

"I can't believe this," Jackie said. "No matter where we are—at home, on a plane over the ocean, here—somehow the note leaver finds us!"

"What I can't believe," Marcia said, grabbing the note from Zinnia's hand and crumpling it into a ball, "is how unreliable the note leaver has become. First the note leaver had no knowledge of Rebecca's superhuman strength, and now the note leaver keeps talking about Zinnia's power when clearly she has none. It's just too much."

"Hey!" Zinnia yelled. "That note was my property!"

All of a sudden, something flew over our heads.

"Hey!" Durinda said. "A carrier pigeon!"

Carrier pigeons often delivered notes to us when we were at home, but it had been quite some time since we'd seen one and we'd certainly never seen one when we *weren't* at home.

Usually when carrier pigeons visited us at home, they went straight to Durinda. Well, perhaps it was because she was almost always the one to open the window and let them inside. But not this time. This time, the carrier pigeon went to Zinnia, landing on her shoulder.

Zinnia turned her head a bit so that she and the carrier pigeon were eye to eye.

"Hello," Zinnia said out loud.

This was odd; usually when Zinnia pretended she could talk to one of our cats, she did so in a whisper.

The carrier pigeon made some sort of noise.

"That's funny," Marcia said. "I didn't think carrier pigeons could talk."

"That's because they can't," Georgia said.

"Better watch it," Rebecca warned Marcia, "or Georgia will start calling you 'you little idiot' too."

"Do you have a name?" Zinnia asked the pigeon.

The pigeon made another sound.

"Did it say Caw?" Annie asked.

"Or was that Kaw?" Jackie suggested.

"Call," Zinnia said. "I see. C'mon, Call, let's go in the cottage."

"Are you going to let her keep that?" Rebecca asked Pete.

"I don't see why not." Pete shrugged. "Besides, we have bigger things to worry about right now, like unpacking all our gear from the car and then getting settled in our new surroundings."

"*New* surroundings," Georgia scoffed softly as we followed Zinnia over the threshold. "More like *old and shabby* surroundings."

Georgia was right for once. The cottage was old and shabby, with dust and cobwebs everywhere, musty sheets covering the furniture.

"Aren't you worried the cats will eat your new pet?" Rebecca asked Zinnia.

"Call's not a pet, it's a friend," Zinnia corrected. "And no. The cats have promised they will not."

We rolled our eyes.

"I knew Annie should have let me buy that birdcage at the store that time," Petal said. "I don't think it's safe to have a pigeon just flying loose indoors willy-nilly."

"C'mon, Call," Zinnia said. "Let's go see the rest of the place."

"I suppose we should be grateful Zinnia didn't name it C'mon," Georgia said. "That would get so annoying."

"Confusing too," Petal added, "because we'd never know who she was talking to any time she said 'C'mon, C'mon'—one of us or the bird."

"No," Rebecca said. "It would just be annoying."

"Hey," Zinnia said to the pigeon as we investigated the room we guessed was supposed to be the living room given its view of the ocean through grimy windows, "did you bring that note for me?"

What a silly question. What did Zinnia think, that the pigeon had come equipped with tape in order to tape her note to the door?

And why was she still talking aloud to it? Was she trying to demonstrate for us her power—you know, the power we all knew she didn't possess?

"Who sent you?" Zinnia asked the pigeon.

The pigeon made a sound. Whatever Zinnia thought that sound meant, it caused her to look confused and then glance around at us.

"That's odd," she said. "Call answered my question by saying 'Zinn.' But that makes no sense. Zinn is the first syllable in my name, and I know *I* didn't send the pigeon to me."

"Maybe Call is just confused," Jackie said kindly. "When the carrier pigeons visit us at home, sometimes they strike their bodies against a window to get attention. Maybe Call accidentally struck its head."

Oh, Jackie, we thought. It's one thing to be kind, but did she really need to go to such great lengths to humor the loony?

"Why don't we go to the kitchen, Call," Zinnia suggested, "and get you a nice cool drink of water?"

"Oh no!" Durinda cried. "Does this place have a . . . *kitchen?*"

"Well," Pete said, looking embarrassed, "you know, it is a cottage, not a hotel, and the man back at the Little Hotel did say something about—"

"Why don't you see if there are any supplies in the kitchen," Rebecca told Durinda. "I'm feeling a bit peckish." She cracked her knuckles. "Still gotta keep my strength up, you know."

"I'm feeling hungry too," Georgia added. "Do you think the previous renters left fixings for chocolate chip pancakes?"

"Perhaps after we unpack and spend a few hours on the beach," Pete said, "I should find a grocery store so we can stock up."

"I *knew* this vacation would somehow result in my cooking!" Durinda fumed.

* * * * * * * *

Once we de-fumed Durinda with promises to help her—it was anyone's guess if we would keep our promises—we set about the business of unpacking the car. Once again, Annie had a clipboard with a manifest attached, this time an unpacking manifest.

"Mr. Pete," Annie directed, "you bring your and Mrs. Pete's suitcases to the biggest bedroom."

"Thanks, pet," Pete said. "It's nice of you to assign us the biggest room."

"Not really," Annie said. "It's just that there's only one biggest room. If one set of four Eights got it, the other set of four would be upset, and there'd be fighting and tears."

"With Petal there's always tears no matter what's going on," Rebecca said.

We ignored Rebecca.

"Georgia, Jackie, and Marcia," Annie directed, "you bring your suitcases to the medium bedroom on the right side of the Petes' bedroom.

"Durinda, Petal, Rebecca, and Zinnia," Annie directed, "you bring your suitcases to the medium bedroom on the left side of the Petes' bedroom. Oh, and Rebecca, since you're the strongest, get mine too and put it in the right-hand bedroom."

"Why can't you carry your own suitcase?" Rebecca objected.

"Someone has to organize things so that everything goes smoothly, doesn't she?" Annie said. "Besides, I thought you enjoyed showing off your strength."

Annie consulted her unpacking manifest.

"Mrs. Pete," Annie directed, we must say in a lot more polite tone than the one she used to direct us, "could you get the bag with the beach items in it so we'll be ready to go just as soon we do a few other things here?"

"What do you mean by 'a few other things'?" Georgia said. "We're nearly done unpacking. Why can't we go as soon as we're done?"

Annie ignored Georgia, which gave us pause. What could Annie be referring to with her 'few other things'?

It was ominous. And while we'd grown accustomed to ominous things from evil persons and others outside our immediate circle of friends, we hated the idea of something ominous coming from a family member.

"Where do you want Daddy Sparky and Mommy Sally?" Pete asked, one under each arm. Apparently, while we were talking, Pete had anticipated the next item on Annie's unpacking manifest.

Annie tapped the end of her pen against her lower lip thoughtfully. We thought it showed her ability to think like an adult that she didn't tap with the nib of the pen, which would no doubt have resulted in blue lips.

"I think," Annie said at last, "that you should pose them in those two comfy chairs in front of the sliding glass doors. That way they can have a prime view of us when we play later on the beach — you know, after we finish doing a few other things."

What *other things?*

"It's not really possible to sit the suit of armor down in a chair," Pete called over, "but the dressmaker's dummy is very bendy." Pete brushed off his hands. "There, that's done," he said cheerily. "I think that's everything from the car."

"It can't be everything," Annie said, looking panicked as she consulted her unpacking manifest. "What about that box I asked you to pack?"

"Oh, right," Pete said, striking the heel of his palm against his forehead. We hoped he hadn't hurt himself. "How could I have forgotten that heavy box?"

As Pete went to fetch it, we wondered what it could

contain. Mentally, we ticked off items on our own unpacking manifests: bathing suits, flip-flops, towels, sunglasses, hats, sunscreen, toothbrushes and toothpaste, shorts and T-shirts, one dress each in case a fancy occasion arose, pajamas, slippers, things with which to entertain ourselves. We already had everything we needed, we thought. So what could be in that box?

We didn't have to wonder much longer, because just then Pete returned, lugging the item in question.

"Where do you want it?" Pete asked Annie.

"Anywhere is fine," Annie said.

As soon as Pete set it down, Annie yanked open the top.

"There!" she said happily, pulling out a very large book—the size of a coloring book, only about five hundred pages long—and placing it beside her, giving it a happy pat as though greeting an old friend. Then she pulled out a second copy of the exact same book and handed it to Durinda.

Durinda turned pale when she saw what she had been given.

The same thing happened with Georgia, Jackie, Marcia, Rebecca, and Zinnia.

The same thing also happened with Petal, except Petal added the bloodcurdling shriek "Oh no! *Not Summer Workbook!*"

And then she fainted.

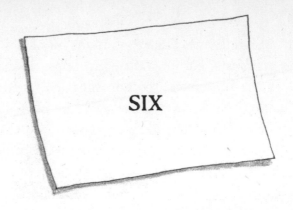

SIX

"Could someone please tell me what *Summer Workbook* is," Pete said, as Durinda and Jackie and Mrs. Pete fanned Petal back to consciousness, "and why its appearance here has managed to knock out Petal?"

"*Summer Workbook* is something our mother has us do," Marcia informed him.

"It's a workbook," Georgia said. "She has us do it every summer. That's why it's called *Summer Workbook*."

"She started this when we were very young," Zinnia said. "Sometimes I tell myself that *Summer Workbook* is like getting a present."

"Well, *I* don't tell myself that," Rebecca said. "In fact, I've told myself that the only good thing about this whole mess we've been in since New Year's Eve is that at least there won't be anyone around to make us do *Summer Workbook*." Rebecca made a disgusted face and added, "There's that dream out the window."

At all those repeated mentions of *Summer Workbook,* Petal fainted again.

More fanning on the parts of Durinda, Jackie, and Mrs. Pete. We hoped their arms weren't getting tired.

"I still don't understand," Pete said. Pete indicated the book next to Annie's side. "Can I see that, please?"

With reluctance, Annie handed it over.

"Summer Workbook." Pete read the title slowly, then he opened the cover and began paging through the book, reading out chapter headings along the way: "'Language Arts,' 'Spelling and Punctuation,' 'Reading Comprehension,' 'Vocabulary,' 'Mathematics,' 'Sample Tests.'" He flipped the book shut and studied the cover. "Hang on," he said. "It says here 'Grade Four.'" He looked up at us. "Isn't that the grade you're entering?"

"Yes," Annie said.

"I don't get it, then," Pete said. "Why would you spend the summer before fourth grade studying everything you're going to learn *in* fourth grade?"

"Don't you see?" Annie said. "That's the beauty of Mommy. Why do you think we're all so smart?" Annie cast a glance at Petal before adding, "Well, most of us. It's because each summer we go through the complete workbook for the grade we're about to enter. That's why we can keep up with our classmates so easily, even though they're all a year older than we are."

They're all—we had to silently chuckle at that. *All* constituted exactly two people, Will Simms and Mandy Stenko.

We sighed. We missed Will Simms. It would be nice to see him again before school started.

"Mommy always said," Jackie said, "that the smarter we became, the better our chances of taking over the world."

"And Daddy always said," Marcia added, "that it's important to have superior math skills so that if you get a modeling contract, you'll be able to know right away if someone is cheating you."

"Plus it's fun being smart," Annie said. "Both Mommy and Daddy said that."

"That all sounds like eminently sensible advice,"

Pete said, "but how long is this *Summer Workbook*? It looks like it's at least five hundred pages."

"It's actually five hundred and three," Annie said, "if you include the index."

"And you expect," Pete said, "yourself and your sisters to get through five hundred and three pages of *Summer Workbook* by the time you go back to school in—what—one month from now?"

"We go back to school on September second," Marcia corrected, "so actually it's a month from yesterday."

"I can't believe it's already August third," Zinnia said. "In just four weeks, it'll be August thirty-first. By then we should know what happened to Mommy and Daddy. Four weeks—it just seems both so long and so short away."

We ignored Zinnia.

"Normally," Annie said, "we'd have the whole summer to get the pages done. Mommy let us have the first week of summer vacation off, but then we'd do enough each day to get it done by September."

"Well," Pete said, "getting five hundred and three pages done in three months is a lot more reasonable than getting it done in one."

"I do know that," Annie said, looking guilty and then looking angry over being made to feel guilty. "But it's not really my fault. We were so busy in June and July, what with weddings and things getting set on fire and then needing to be put out, that I forgot all about it. But then, right when we decided to come to the Seaside, I remembered. That's why I went out to get the books."

At the mention of the word *Seaside,* seven Eights perked up.

We were at the Seaside . . . and the beach was right outside!

"Let's go swimming!" Zinnia said.

For once, we were all in agreement with Zinnia. Well, most of us were.

"We can't go *swimming* right now!" Annie was outraged. "We need to do *Summer Workbook*!"

"Not right this minute, we don't," Rebecca said, folding her arms across her chest. "I'm staging a revolt."

For once, we were all in agreement with Rebecca too.

"I revolt!" Durinda said.

"I revolt!" Georgia said.

"I revolt!" Jackie said.

"I revolt!" Marcia said.

"I revolt!" Petal said. Then she added, "Even though I'm not sure what that means."

"I revolt!" Zinnia said. "Let's go swimming!"

"But we have only thirty days to get through five hundred and three pages!" Annie said. "How many pages does that come to a day, Marcia? Quick, do the math."

"It comes to sixteen point seven six six, and on for as long as you can see sixes, pages," Marcia said. Then she saw fit to observe, "It would have been only five point five eight eight pages per day if you'd remembered to remind us to do *Summer Workbook* as soon as summer vacation began."

"Don't you see the urgency of the situation?" Annie said, appealing to Pete.

Apparently Annie thought she could drag an adult along for the ride in her madness. But Pete refused to be dragged.

"Sorry, pet," Pete said, "but I'm afraid I have to side with the revolters."

"But—" Annie started to protest, but Pete held up a hand, cutting her off. Some of us thought she was about to say that *revolters* wasn't a real word. It was, though. Some of us were very good with the vocabulary sections each summer.

"No buts," Pete said. "We came here to have a proper vacation, and a proper vacation we shall have. Now then." He clapped his hands. "All of you into your bathing suits."

Annie hung her head. Even Annie knew that you could appeal to an adult but you couldn't overrule one, not if the adult was Pete.

"Oh, don't look so glum, Annie," Pete said. "I promise, after we have a day of fun at the beach and a nice dinner and then perhaps some more fun, if you want to make your sisters do sixteen point seven six six and so on pages of *Summer Workbook* before retiring for the night, you just go for it."

LAST RESORT

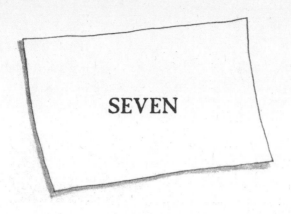

SEVEN

We were all ready for the beach. We were standing on the deck and we had our bathing suits on, some of us in one-piece suits, some in bikinis. Well, Pete wasn't wearing a one-piece or a bikini. But he did have an inner tube in the shape of a sea serpent wrapped around his waist.

"I'm not much on swimming as such," Pete said when we looked pointedly at his serpent. "I prefer to just bob in the water."

We decided not to comment on the fact that Pete was wearing his work boots.

In addition to our bathing suits, we wore sunscreen, and we were carrying our towels. We also carried five beach umbrellas: Annie and Durinda had one, Georgia and Rebecca another, Jackie and Marcia a third, the Petes a fourth, and Zinnia struggled with one on her own, which was not easy to do with Call on one shoulder.

Poor Zinnia was struggling because one of us had yet to show up.

"Petal," Pete called into the house, "I'd hate to do anything to upset you, and I certainly wouldn't want to do anything to cause you to faint right now, but just what is taking you so long?"

We waited. And waited. And waited.

At last, at *long* last, Petal appeared.

Well, we assumed it was Petal inside and under all of that, but it was just an assumption.

"Petal?" Pete asked. "Is that you in there? And if so, what *are* you wearing?"

"I have on SPF one hundred plus zinc oxide on my nose," Petal said. "I have a floppy hat on my head, but I've also put sunscreen on the part in my hair and all around my ears, just in case. I am wearing a bathing suit from the early part of the nineteen hundreds, for modesty's sake; a towel wrapped around that; and a full-length terry-cloth robe over that. On my feet I have flip-flops, but I put my bunny slippers over those because the flip-flops don't give enough coverage. Oh, and I have on big dark sunglasses with the strongest UVF protection available."

"I have only one question," Pete said. "Why?"

"Because I don't want to burn, do I," Petal said. "You're not going to catch me exposing an inch of skin to the Seaside sun—not one inch! The Seaside sun, as everyone knows, is a very dangerous thing."

"You look like a mummy," Georgia said. "And your cat—poor Precious. Can Precious really breathe all wrapped up like that?"

"I knew it," Rebecca said. "I knew it!" She groaned. "This is going to be yet another of those vacations where everyone who sees us thinks we're all out of our tiny little minds, isn't it?"

* * * * * * * *

We settled ourselves on towels under our respective beach umbrellas, all except for Zinnia, who sat up and talked to Call.

Well, of course she did.

"Are there really eight Other Eights," Zinnia asked Call, "and where are they from?"

We had no idea why Zinnia would assume that Call knew a thing about the Other Eights. More crazy talk as far as we were concerned.

"Are they from Pittsburgh?" Zinnia persisted. "Vietnam? Spain? I'm almost certain they can't be from France. If they were, they'd have been at the wedding of Aunt Martha and Uncle George."

"Ask Call if they're from England, like Annie's faux-Daddy accent," Rebecca suggested.

"Ha! Ha!" Georgia said.

"You shouldn't mock Zinnia like that," Jackie said. "She can't help being the way she is. It's just too much for one person: all of the stress of being the only Eight to have to get her power and gift in the same month we all have our eighth birthday and after which we're supposed to discover how Mommy and Daddy disappeared."

"Or died," Rebecca put in.

"It's just too much stress for one Eight," Jackie stressed again, ignoring Rebecca. "No wonder Zinnia feels the need to acquire pigeon pets and pretend she can talk to those same pigeon pets."

"I heard that, Jackie," Zinnia said. Shockingly, her voice lacked a tone of offense as she added, "And it's not a pigeon pet. I keep telling you, it's a pigeon friend."

"I'm sorry," Jackie said.

"That's okay," Zinnia said.

"Why be sorry?" Georgia said. "And why is it okay? All any of this is is more crazy talk!"

"Has anyone else noticed," Jackie said, "that whenever we're all together, which is pretty much every minute of our waking lives, all we do is make fun of one another?"

"Oh, come on, Jackie," Durinda said. "We do support each other sometimes. It's not that bad."

Jackie thought about this for a moment.

"Yes," she finally said. "I really do think it is that bad." Then she grew excited. "I know!" she said. "I propose we spend a half an hour — no, a full hour — during which all we say is kind things about one another. Anyone else game?"

We didn't know if we were game, not exactly. But those waves in the ocean looked very choppy. So, sure. We were willing to play along.

"Okay," Jackie said excitedly, "who's ready to go first?"

Well, when she put it like *that* . . .

"Fine," Jackie said when it was clear no one was going to volunteer, "I'll go first. And I'll say that . . . let's see . . . that Georgia's naturally curly hair is most attractive on her. And further, when Georgia puts her mind to it, she can be quite sweet."

"Thanks, Jackie," Georgia said, "although it did sound as though you had to reach for that last part. Looks as though we're playing upward, meaning we're supposed to say something nice about the Eight in birth order ahead of us. That should be easy. Durinda makes a mean chocolate chip pancake. Phew, I'm glad that's over. It's not so easy being nice for an extended period of time."

"I may not always agree with Annie's tactics," Durinda contributed, "but I respect the fact that since New Year's Eve she's run this family pretty much as well as any adult could."

"Zinnia is sweet," Annie said, "probably the sweetest Eight we've got, but I do worry about this thinking-she-can-talk-to-cats-and-birds thing. That can't be healthy."

Zinnia was kind enough to ignore that last part, merely saying, "Rebecca is not nearly as nasty as she pretends to be."

Whenever one of us was called upon to say something nice about Rebecca, this not-nearly-as-nasty-as-she-pretends-to-be thing was pretty much all we could come up with. We didn't say it because we knew it was true; it was more because we hoped it might be.

"Great," Rebecca said. "That's just great. How am I supposed to follow that high praise?" She turned to Petal in her mummy costume. "I'm sorry!" Rebecca cried at last. "But I just can't do it! How can you expect me to say something positive about *that?*"

We looked where she was looking, at Petal. We kind of did understand what Rebecca meant.

"Fine," Petal said, rising to her feet as best she could in her mummy costume. "If no one can think of anything nice to say about me, I'll take myself off for a bit. I'll . . . I'll . . . I'll go for a walk."

And off Petal walked, as best she could.

"Well, that's just great," Jackie said, looking dejected as Petal trudged away in her bunny slippers through the sand. "We couldn't get through one whole round of the family being nice to one another without one of us saying something insulting, never mind lasting a whole hour. How long did we last, a whole five minutes?"

"Maybe it was six," Zinnia said optimistically.

"Actually, I'm fairly certain it was five minutes and twenty-seven seconds," Marcia said, apparently consulting some internal clock that was extremely precise. Then she frowned. "Or was that twenty-eight seconds?"

"We're sorry, Jackie," Durinda said. "And here, no one even got the chance to say anything nice about you."

"Or me," Marcia added.

"I don't care," Jackie said, and we could tell she didn't. Jackie was just like that. "But look at Petal."

We looked. There went Petal, trudging farther and farther away from us in her bunny slippers. Why, she was so far away, she practically looked like a normal person.

"Back home," Jackie went on, "Petal sometimes asks for an escort just to go to the bathroom—and it's our bathroom in our house! And now here she is going off by herself without any family protection. Where *can* she be going?"

* * * * * * * *

A half-hour later, or what seemed like a half-hour, Petal trudged back, breathless.

"Petal," Jackie said, "what's wrong?"

"Someone was following me," Petal said, still trying to catch her breath.

"Following you?" seven Eights plus the Petes cried in concern. "But who? Why?"

"If I knew that," Petal said, "I would tell you. All I know is, every time I took a step, the shadow behind me took a step too." Petal paused and then burst out with "I have a stalker!"

Oh, Petal.

"Oh, Petal," even Jackie felt forced to say. "Of course you don't have a stalker. You must be seeing your own shadow. Why, look how low the sun is in the sky."

Petal looked, stopped, wondered.

"There's the positive thing I have to say about Petal," Rebecca said. "Petal's so scared of everything, she's scared of her own shadow. I don't know about the rest of you, but I think it's kind of *cute!*"

And so ended the first full day of our vacation, August 3. Well, we did have a bonfire on the beach, over which we cooked fish dogs and toasted marshmallows— Pete found a Seaside store where he could do a Big Shop—and Petal worried that the bonfire would kill us all, and then we went back to our rooms and did 16.766 pages of various parts of the workbook, just to please Annie and because we liked to skip around in *Summer Workbook,* and then we went to sleep.

But really, we would think later, the day might just as well have ended when Rebecca insulted Petal by assuming that Petal was merely scared of her own shadow.

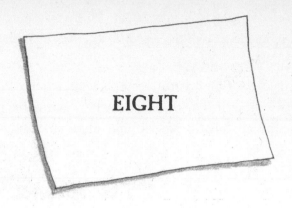

EIGHT

It was the next morning, August 4.

"I'm hungry!" Annie announced.

"I'm hungry!" Georgia announced.

"I'm hungry!" Jackie announced.

"I'm hungry!" Marcia announced.

"I'm hungry!" Petal announced.

"I'm hungry!" Rebecca announced.

"I'm hungry!" Zinnia announced.

"I must say," Pete said, patting his belly, "I'm a bit hungry myself."

"It's odd," Mrs. Pete added, "but fish dogs don't stick with a person as long as a person might think they would."

"Well, don't look at me," Durinda said. "I'm not going to make everyone's breakfast. It's supposed to be my vacation too, after all."

We all turned to Jackie, sure she'd bail us out. And we were sure she was about to, since she was smiling and had opened her mouth to speak. But before any words could come out, someone else spoke.

"Fine," Georgia said. "I'll make breakfast for everybody."

We gaped at her. *Georgia— Georgia,* who never did anything resembling a chore unless sternly commanded to by Annie—was offering to make us all breakfast?

Our gaping continued as Georgia headed into the kitchen, and our gaping continued yet further at the ensuing racket that came from that room. The sound of cabinets opening and slamming shut, drawers being yanked out and slid in, the clatter of crockery, and the tinkling of silverware.

"She must be making us a feast in there," Annie said in a hushed voice.

"What's that other sound?" Jackie asked.

"Is Georgia humming?" Petal asked.

"No," Marcia corrected. "She's whistling. Georgia's whistling while she's working."

"Huh," Durinda said, sounding miffed. "I never whistle while I work."

"Is everyone ready for breakfast?" Georgia shouted to us.

We don't feel the need to recount our individual responses here. Suffice to say that basically we all shouted back, "Yes!"

"Ready or not," Georgia called, "here comes breakfast!"

A moment later Georgia emerged from the kitchen bearing a tray upon which sat two bowls, two spoons, a box, and ten juice boxes. She handed the bowls, which we now saw contained cereal, to the Petes and the box to Annie.

"Sorry," Georgia said, "but the little cottage doesn't come with service for ten, so I figured it was only fair that the Petes get the two bowls, since they are old."

"Old*er*," Annie corrected with a smile toward the Petes, as though to prove the rest of us weren't as bad as, well, Georgia. "Georgia just means you're older than us and therefore worthy of respect."

Good save, Annie!

"What's this feast you've prepared for us?" Rebecca demanded of Georgia as we each reached for a juice box, pleased to see it was mango.

"Razzle Crunchies, of course," Georgia said, "the official cereal of the Sisters Eight."

"You made all that noise in the kitchen," Durinda said, "just to wind up serving us a box of Razzle Crunchies?"

"It was a very involved process," Georgia said. "Anyway, I thought it was rather wonderful that Mr. Pete was able to find Razzle Crunchies at the little Seaside grocery store. I always assumed Razzle Crunchies were a delicacy available for sale only in the town where we live. Now, eat up, everybody, so we can get to the beach."

"But how are we supposed to eat up," Rebecca said, "when the Petes are the only ones with bowls and Annie's holding the box?"

"Oh, right," Georgia said. "Well, since there are only two bowls, we're supposed to just pass the box among ourselves and shove our hands in and grab what we like." Georgia turned to Annie. "Do you think you could stop hogging the box now?"

"Sor*ry*," Annie said, grabbing a handful and handing the box to Durinda, who accepted the box grudgingly.

"When *I* make breakfast," Durinda muttered, "it doesn't go like this."

"Um, terrific breakfast, Georgia," Pete said politely around a mouthful of Razzle and Crunch.

"Where's Call?" Zinnia said suddenly, looking worried. "I haven't seen him since last night. Call! Call!"

"Oh no," Petal said. "Call is probably one of those traitor pigeon pets you're always hearing about in the news. Probably right this minute Call is off somewhere trading our secrets with the enemy in exchange for better pigeon food."

We ignored Petal.

"Call! Call!" Zinnia shouted as she moved from room to room.

We wished we could ignore Zinnia too, and we would have if she hadn't been shouting so loudly.

"Call! Ca—"

"Oh, good," Jackie said. "Zinnia must have found Call, because she's stopped shouting."

"Or else she found Call dead," Rebecca added, then added some more. "Or else Zinnia's dead."

But as it turned out, neither dire outcome was the case, which we saw when Zinnia entered with Call perched on her shoulder.

"Where did you find Call?" Jackie asked.

"Outside," Zinnia said happily, "with the cats. Call and Zither were having a conversation. I think they were trying to get to know each other better."

Oh, Zinnia.

* * * * * * * *

"Isn't anyone going in the water?" Pete asked.

We were back on the beach again, in the same spot we'd been in the day before. We all had our bathing suits on, except for Petal, who had on—well, you know.

"I said," Pete said, "isn't anyone going in the water? No one went in yesterday."

We ignored Pete, although what he said was true. We hadn't gone in yesterday, and we weren't going in today, because, well, we were somewhat scared of the water here. Back home, we didn't have an ocean. Back home, all we had was a wading pool we'd outgrown and that had never been scary in the first place, except maybe to Petal. But this, this . . . *ocean*—it was so vast. We couldn't even see where it ended. We were scared of things we couldn't see the end of, the great uncertainty of it all.

"This is so odd," Pete said. "Why come to the Seaside and then just sit by the side part and not go in the sea part?"

"But there are plenty of other things to do by the side of the sea," Annie pointed out.

"Things that are even more fun than actually going into the sea," Durinda added.

"Like what?" Pete said.

"We could play beach volleyball," Jackie suggested.

"I'm fairly certain that's something people do at the side of the sea," Marcia added.

"Do you see a volleyball or a net anywhere?" Georgia scoffed.

We didn't mind so much her scoffing at Marcia, but we rather did mind her scoffing at Jackie.

"Why don't we bury Petal up to her neck in the sand?" Rebecca suggested. "Burying people up to their necks in the sand is definitely a by-the-sea activity, and anyway, with all the clothes Petal's wearing, she's practically buried already."

"Oh no," Petal said forcefully. "You won't catch me letting myself be buried in the sand. That's a terribly dangerous thing for a person to allow to happen to herself. A passing pigeon might think my head was a perch, and then where would I be? I'd be known as Petal the Pigeon Perch. It would be so embarrassing."

We didn't think anything could be more embarrassing than the outfit Petal was wearing.

"Or else," Petal went on, "you might bury me and then all decide you wanted to get snow cones. So you'd run off to do that, leaving me here alone, and then you wouldn't be able to find me again later because all I'd be is a tiny head in the crowd and I'd be stuck here the rest of my life."

We hadn't thought the fear of being a pigeon perch could be topped, but somehow she'd managed to do it.

"Or else—" Petal started in on yet another new fear, but Rebecca cut her off.

"Fine," Rebecca said. "You can all bury me, then. I don't mind. *I* think it would be rather fun to be buried."

So that's what we did, buried Rebecca up to her neck in the sand. We had to admit: burying Rebecca was rather fun. In fact, we wondered why we hadn't thought of it earlier.

"Now what?" Georgia asked, once Rebecca was entirely covered up to her neck, only her head remaining visible. "Do we just sit around here and stare at your head all day, Rebecca? The burying part was fun but I don't see staring at your head all day as being much of a game."

"I think," Zinnia said, slowly rising to her feet, "I'll take a little dip in the ocean."

What?

"What?" Pete said.

We hadn't told Pete about our fear—of course we hadn't told him that—but the tone of his voice told us we'd picked up on it on his own. It was funny how Pete could be intelligent like that at times.

"It'll just be a little dip," Zinnia said, heading toward the water's edge. "I shouldn't be too long."

"Don't go too far!" Pete shouted after her. "Do you

see those buoys bobbing a little ways out? Don't go past that line!"

Without turning, Zinnia waved her hand in the air, acknowledging that she'd heard Pete.

We watched with interest as Zinnia stood at the edge of the water and got her toes wet. We watched with interest as she kicked at the water playfully with her feet. We watched with interest as she began walking out into the water, jumping over tiny waves as they came at her.

"Don't go too far out!" Pete shouted again, rising to his feet as Zinnia waded farther into the ocean.

We'd been doing a lot of watching with interest, but now we watched in horror as a dark shape beneath the surface of the water made straight for Zinnia.

"Oh no!" Petal shouted. "It's a shark!"

"Shark!" Pete shouted, running toward the water. "Zinnia, get out of the water!"

"Shark!" we all shouted, including Mrs. Pete, as we all ran after Pete.

"Shark!" Rebecca's head shouted.

We'd never run so fast in our lives, and as we ran, we saw more dark shapes beneath the surface heading straight for Zinnia. But why wasn't Zinnia moving? Why wasn't she running from the ocean? Why wasn't she trying to save herself?

And then, as we plunged into the surf, heedless of the danger to ourselves in our quest to save Zinnia, we saw that the dark shapes weren't sharks at all.

We froze where we were, stared.

Under a sky so perfectly blue it might have been colored with one of the crayons from our box back home, and as the sunlight shimmered on the ocean, making sparkling diamond spots on the green waves, we saw that what we'd thought were sharks were dolphins, all swimming around Zinnia as though she were one of them.

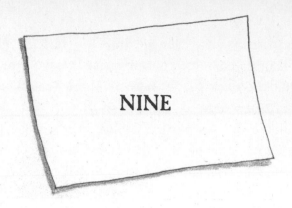

NINE

Pete let out a low whistle.

"I'd never believe this," Pete said, "if I weren't seeing it with my own eyes."

We'd heard Pete say similar things on a few previous occasions, whenever he witnessed the results of one of us getting her power.

Well, we knew this couldn't be that. This was simply . . . whatever it was.

"Dolphins don't typically come in this close to the shore," Pete said.

"I wouldn't have thought they could," Mrs. Pete said.

We ignored the Petes, overcoming our frozen state to join Zinnia amid the dolphins.

"What about me?" Rebecca's head shouted to us.

We ignored Rebecca's head too.

We'd heard the word *frolic* before, but we couldn't say it was an activity any of us had ever engaged in. We did so now, however, frolicking in the ocean with

Zinnia and the dolphins and even the Petes, who were frolicking too.

The dolphins were so beautiful, with their gray skin and their wide mouths that looked like great big smiles. And they were so friendly too. They did seem to like Zinnia better than they liked the rest of us put together, but they didn't entirely ignore us. In fact, they let us pet them, and they didn't spit on us, so we figured they must like us well enough.

"What about me?" Rebecca's head shouted.

"These may not be sharks," Petal said, suddenly sounding worried, "but what's that black thing heading toward us?"

We looked up in time to see the dark fin snaking its way to us.

Now we froze in fear.

All except for Zinnia, that is, who tilted her head to one side, frowning at the approaching fin.

The fin abruptly ceased approaching, turned, and headed out to sea again.

"How odd," Annie said as we all relaxed.

"How lucky," Durinda said.

Zinnia said nothing.

"This is so much fun," Jackie said, petting a dolphin.

"Almost as much fun as getting caught in an avalanche," Georgia admitted.

"I wonder how many dolphins there are here," Marcia said. "Maybe I should count them?"

"I would like to stay and keep doing this," Petal said, "but the water has waterlogged my bathrobe and all the other clothes I've got on, and I do believe I'm about to slip beneath the surface and drown."

It was a testament to how peaceful it was being surrounded by dolphins who were so gentle they were willing to frolic with us that Petal said this in such an even tone of voice. Why, she hardly sounded scared at all. Perhaps she was just joking.

But when we turned to look at her, we could see she was barely keeping her head above the water.

"Petal!" Annie cried. Then she turned to us. "Quick, we have to get Petal out of here!"

Five of us plus the Petes clasped our arms together under Petal to create a stretcher upon which to carry her out.

"It looks like you've got that under control," Zinnia said from her place among the dolphins. "Does anyone mind if I just stay out here for a few more minutes?"

* * * * * * * *

A few more minutes later, Zinnia was still in the water while the rest of us had finished dragging the sodden

Petal back and had placed her on a spot under our beach umbrellas.

Well, all of us except for one, and by *one* we don't mean Zinnia . . .

"How inconsiderate!" Rebecca's head snapped at us. "You all went off to . . . *frolic,* and you left me here by myself in the sand. You could have dug me out first."

"You know you could have used your own superhuman strength to dig yourself out of the sand," Georgia countered.

"Huh," Rebecca said. "I hadn't even thought of that."

"Besides," Jackie said, "it's not like it would have been nice for us to stop to dig you out when we thought Zinnia was about to get eaten by a shark."

"What does *nice* have to do with anything?" Rebecca said.

"What's this?" Marcia said.

"What's what?" Rebecca said.

"Behind your head," Marcia said. "There's what looks suspiciously like a note here."

"Well, how could I have seen it if it's *behind* my head?" Rebecca said.

"But didn't you hear anyone come up behind you and leave it there?" Annie said.

We saw the sand around Rebecca ripple and realized she'd just shrugged, exercising her superhuman strength against the weight of the sand. In fact, she'd shrugged so hard, she'd shrugged her shoulders free, and soon she pulled her arms out as well.

"I was too busy watching you all—first running and then freezing and then frolicking and then freezing again and so forth—to notice what was going on behind me," Rebecca said.

"Oh no!" Marcia cried, ignoring Rebecca.

Huh, we thought. "Oh no!" was usually Petal's line.

"Oh no!" Marcia cried again, and now we could see that she'd opened the note and was reading it. She read it to us:

Dear Zinnia,

Still enjoying your power, I see— good show!

"The note leaver is still acting all kerflooey," Marcia said. "We all know that this isn't Zinnia's power, that this thing with the dolphins is just—I don't know— *something else,* but the note leaver keeps acting like it *is* her power."

We looked from the note to Zinnia frolicking with the dolphins. We knew Marcia was right. Zinnia couldn't communicate with animals. They just liked her. That's all it was.

"Oh, we can't let Zinnia see this," Marcia said.

"But it was addressed to her," Annie said.

"I agree with Marcia," Rebecca said, pulling herself all the way out of the sand. "Zinnia's always been the nuttiest Eight." Rebecca paused to look at Petal, who was on all fours shaking back and forth in her bathrobe like a dog trying to rid itself of water, which she had plenty of right now. "Well, one of the two nuttiest Eights," Rebecca corrected herself. "Always believing she could talk to the cats, then thinking she could talk to that stupid pigeon pet, and now this thing with the dolphins. On top of that, there're these notes that keep coming, talking about her power. If she sees this latest one, right after that thing with the dolphins, we'll never be able to convince her that she *can't* communicate with animals. And if she goes on believing she *can* communicate with animals, eventually she'll be labeled crazy, we'll have to lock her away in a lunatic asylum, and there goes the whole family reputation."

"I think that ship has sailed," Jackie said, "on more than one voyage."

"My, that was a long speech," Georgia said to Rebecca.

"Yes, well," Rebecca said, "a person has a long time to think when she's buried up to her head in sand all alone while everyone else is playing."

"But you didn't know about the note at that time,"

Georgia said, "so how could you have been thinking this out then?"

"I wasn't," Rebecca said. She shrugged. "I guess it's just the leftover effects from before of having more time on my hands to think. My brain must still be doing that."

"Never mind all that right now," Marcia said, exasperated. "Who cares what Rebecca's brain is doing? The important thing is to get this note away from here before Zinnia comes back and sees it."

"You'd better hurry, then," Georgia said, looking toward the ocean, "because she's coming out now."

We looked up in time to see Zinnia wave to the dolphins before turning in our direction.

"Oh," Petal said, sounding exasperated as she struggled to her feet, "I'll take it."

"*You'll* take it?"

Okay, we all said that, including the Petes. We were that shocked: Petal offering to go off by herself again, Petal volunteering for a mission.

"What's wrong with that?" Petal said. "I did manage to walk by myself yesterday without disaster striking. Well, there was that little problem with the shadow, but since you did all convince me it was just my own . . ." Petal held her hand out for Marcia to give her the note. "Besides," Petal added, shaking her arms, "the walk will do me good. Maybe I'll finally be able to lose the rest of this water weight."

* * * * * * *

"What have you all been up to?" Zinnia asked, joining us a moment later.

The words Zinnia spoke were innocent enough in and of themselves, and even the way she delivered them sounded perfectly normal.

Still, we couldn't escape the sense of guilt washing over us as we kicked the sand with our feet, hands clasped behind our backs.

"Nothing much," we said, hoping we sounded innocent too.

* * * * * * *

Petal didn't sound at all innocent when she returned to us. She sounded frightened. And angry.

"You were all wrong," she said. "There was somebody following me yesterday. I know that because the same person followed me today."

Oh, Petal.

"It's true," she insisted, reading our Oh-Petal expressions accurately. "I went a ways down the beach to bury"—she paused, cast a look at Zinnia—"you know, something unimportant in the sand. Walking there I didn't notice anything funny, probably because my mind was occupied by my mission." She cast another glance at Zinnia, adding, "My thoroughly unimportant mission. But on my way back, when my mind was no longer occupied, I saw the shadow again."

"We already explained to you yesterday," Annie pointed out with a surprising degree of patience, "that's your own shadow."

"No, it's not," Petal said. "I took my own shadow into account, and this shadow wasn't my shadow. Every time I'd take a step, my shadow and this other shadow would take a step too. Every time I stopped taking steps, my shadow and this other shadow would also stop. Whenever I tried to turn around, though, to catch the person in the act, I couldn't see anybody behind me. Whoever this shadow person is, he or she must be very fast and good at hiding. Anyway, my shadow and this other shadow followed me all the way here."

We all craned our necks to peer around Petal.

"Well," Pete said gently, "if another shadow followed you all the way here, it must have escaped fairly quickly and been invisible in the first place, because you're the only one standing in front of us and there's no second shadow behind you."

"Perhaps," Mrs. Pete suggested, just as gently, "you've spent too much time overdressed in the sun, dear?"

"I know what I saw," Petal said, turning in circles to try to catch this imaginary other shadow, "even if none of you see it now and I don't either. What if it's someone dangerous that's following me in the hopes of worming secrets out of me? What if it's Bill Collector or, worse, what if it's finally the ax murderer? What if—"

"We'll all go for a walk with you this time," Annie suggested. "We'll walk with you and we'll keep count of all our shadows as we walk. If someone is following you—or us—we'll catch that person."

We expected Rebecca to say something snide about Annie humoring the loony, but she didn't. We figured that for once Rebecca had seen the wisdom of Annie's ways and recognized the fact that Annie was right: if we didn't do something to humor the loony, and fast, Petal would never stop going on about this.

* * * * * * * *

So we walked.

We walked, and walked, and walked.

"We have ten shadows," Annie had announced heartily when we first started walking. But as the day went on, and the walking continued, the heartiness of those announcements waned to something less enthusiastic, like "Yup, still just ten shadows."

"Can we stop for a snack?" Georgia said.

"Is it tomorrow yet?" Rebecca said. "Perhaps this is all just one big nightmare I'm having."

"I don't like to complain," Zinnia said, "but my feet are getting a bit tired."

"Maybe—" Jackie started to say.

We never did learn what sensible Jackie had to contribute because just then Petal said in an urgent whisper, "There it is! There's the shadow!"

We stopped walking and began counting shadows. We counted again.

Petal was right: there *was* an eleventh shadow!

"It's the same shadow I saw yesterday and today," Petal whispered, still urgently. "And as you can see, it's nothing like my shadow."

It was true. This eleventh shadow had nowhere near the bulk of Petal's bathrobe shadow.

Ten heads swiveled around abruptly. We admit it, we half expected to see no one there, just as Petal said happened every time she tried to catch the person following her. We half expected to learn there was nothing following us but a mysterious shadow, which would have been scary in its own way.

How funny, then, to turn around and see . . .

"A *boy?*" Annie said.

There was a boy behind us, and no one else in sight. Or at least not in sight behind us. The boy had on a bathing suit and sandals. He had brown hair and brown eyes, kind of like us. If we had to say how tall he was, we'd have said he was closest to Georgia in height. In fact, his hair was most similar to Georgia's as well.

The boy was smiling at us.

"Who are you?" Annie demanded.

"George," the boy said, still smiling.

That seemed odd. *George . . . Georgia . . .*

"Have you been following Petal?" Annie said, still using her demanding voice.

"I might have been," the boy named George said, still smiling, "but not for anything bad." Abruptly, he raised his hand, waved. "See you around!"

And then he turned and raced away from us down the beach, his body becoming smaller and smaller until it was finally invisible as the orange sun disappeared from the sky.

"Huh," Annie said, hands on hips. "What do you think that was all about?"

"Maybe he has a crush on Petal," Durinda suggested.

Rebecca looked at Petal, snorted. "You cannot be serious."

We couldn't help it. We laughed too. The idea of that boy, the ridiculous idea of any boy, having a crush on Petal when she was wearing her Petal beach getup . . .

It took us a moment to realize one of us wasn't laughing, and by *one of us* we don't mean Petal, who apparently found this as uproarious as the rest of us.

"Whatever that boy George wanted," Zinnia said thoughtfully, "I don't think that was it."

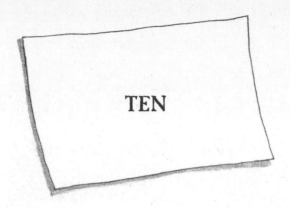

TEN

"No more excuses!" Annie shouted.

"Of course we can come up with more excuses," Rebecca countered. "Just give us time."

It was the following morning, August 5, and we'd finished breakfast and changed into our beach clothes because we were going to the beach right after breakfast.

Or so we thought.

Turned out, Annie had other plans for us.

And those other plans went by the seemingly innocent two-word phrase *Summer Workbook.*

"I don't care what other excuses you might be able to come up with," Annie said now, "because it doesn't matter. Yesterday we were so busy, what with frolicking with dolphins and trying to identify shadows, we never got around to getting our daily quota in. That means we're a full day behind schedule. That means a double dose today if we want to get it all done before school starts."

"But we don't want to get it done," Rebecca said.

"None of us do," Georgia added. "Well, except for you."

"It doesn't matter what you want or don't want," Annie said. "I'm in charge and I say we need to do double. Now then, two times sixteen point seven six six comes to how much?" Annie looked to Marcia.

"Don't tell her!" six Eights shouted at Marcia.

But we needn't have bothered.

"Thirty-three point five three two," Marcia answered promptly. Then she turned to us with an apologetic shrug. "Sorry," she said. "I just can't help myself."

Annie ignored the last part of what Marcia said, responding only to the part that mattered to her.

"That's right," Annie said. "So if we're going to get thirty-three point five three two pages done today, we really do need to—"

"Excuse me," Jackie said, cutting Annie off, which was a brave thing to do. Almost no one cut off Annie. "I don't mean to offend you, Annie, but we've all been wondering: Why are you the way you are?"

It was true. We had been wondering. Not only had we been wondering, but just that morning we'd been discussing it among ourselves while Annie was in the bathroom. At the end of the discussion, we'd nominated Jackie to talk to Annie about it. Okay, we begged Jackie to, because the rest of us were too scared to take Annie on about anything in general and this in particular.

"Excuse me?" Annie said now, sternly.

"It's just that," Jackie said gently, "we do remember what you were like before Mommy and Daddy disappeared. True, you've always been the oldest. And, being the oldest, you did tend to be bossy when compared to, say, Petal. But not like this. Not this constant need to be in charge of every little thing. Not this constant need to control everything we do and make sure everyone does your bidding. I hate to say it, but at times it makes it difficult to like you. We always love you, but this morning you are making liking you very hard. We just want to have a good vacation. Don't you want to have a good vacation too?"

As Jackie spoke, we watched Annie's face change from stern to confused and finally to sad. Even the least observant of us marked these changes. And then that made us sad, not just for Annie but also for Jackie, who we knew never liked to be the cause of sadness in anyone else.

Oh no. Was that a tear in Annie's eye?

"Do you have any idea," Annie said, her voice quavering, "how hard these past seven months and five days have been on me? I knew *someone* had to take charge of leading the family in Mommy's and Daddy's absence, or we'd all get split up. We'd lose each other. I did it because I felt I had to, so our lives wouldn't turn to chaos and ruin. But do you honestly think I enjoy being thought of as the bossy Eight?"

"Yes," Rebecca said, "I do think that."

"That's not helpful," Jackie told Rebecca as she put her arm around Annie.

"You're right," Rebecca said. "I don't honestly think she enjoys being thought of as the bossy Eight. But I do think she enjoys being bossy. A lot."

"That's not helpful either," Jackie said.

"No, no," Annie said, sounding so very sad. "Rebecca's right. Perhaps I have enjoyed it too much, you know, being bossy."

Oh, we hated seeing Annie like this. Seeing Annie looking sad and broken was far worse than having her order us around. We were almost certain that, despite the nasty things she said, even Rebecca felt this way.

After Annie's tears and all that she'd said, we felt we understood her a little better. True, there was some choice in her behavior toward us, but mostly it just had to do with her being her. Why, Annie couldn't stop herself from acting as though she were in charge of everything any more than Marcia could stop herself from blurting out the answer to 2 times 16.766. It was just her nature.

Suddenly, we felt we *had* to do something to make Annie feel good.

"You know, Annie," Zinnia said, "I really do feel like doing *Summer Workbook*."

"If you dry your tears," Petal promised, "I'll get out my *Summer Workbook* right now."

"I know we only just had breakfast a short time ago," Durinda offered, "but I could make us all a snack for extra brainpower while we work."

"I'll go get the pencils," Georgia offered.

"This is great," Marcia said when we all had our pencils and workbooks in front of us. "I *love* doing *Summer Workbook*!"

"There's no need to lay it on quite that thick, Marcia," Rebecca said.

"What are you talking about?" Marcia said. "I *do* love doing *Summer Workbook*." Marcia gave a happy sigh. "I just love learning things."

"Could someone look at my forehead?" Petal said. "I feel as though my brain is expanding already and I am worried it might be beginning to bulge."

Oh, Petal.

Jackie studied the proffered forehead kindly. "No worries," Jackie said. "It looks like your brain is probably still the same size."

Annie cleared her throat. "You do know," she said,

"that I do love all of you and that's partly why I am the way I am, right?"

Yeah. We did know that.

Just then there came a rumble of thunder followed by a downpour of rain, sheets of it.

"That roof never did look sound," Pete said. "I'll go find some buckets to catch the water that's leaking through the ceiling."

While Pete did that, Petal grabbed one of Pete's work boots and placed it under the biggest leak. "Stinky but effective," she pronounced.

It was a good thing, we thought as lightning crackled through the sky, that we hadn't left for the beach.

And it was a good thing, we thought as it continued to rain throughout the day, that we had something with which to keep ourselves occupied inside.

* * * * * * * *

It is funny how summer can affect a person's brain. You go through the school year, learning all sorts of things, and then summer comes and you think: *Well, that's enough of that for now. Yippee!*

But doing *Summer Workbook* that day as a summer storm raged outside reminded us of all we'd been missing, the excitement of learning about new things a person hadn't even dreamed existed.

By the time Zinnia lifted her head up, we'd long passed the combined quota for that day and the day before, and none of us had complained about all the work we were doing, not once, not even Rebecca. Perhaps we hadn't complained because we were too busy having fun seeing how much we did know and how much we could know.

"What's this?" Zinnia asked, her finger marking a spot on the page.

We all gathered round Zinnia and saw that she was working in the Mathematics section.

"It's an infinity symbol," Annie said.

"Yes, I know that," Zinnia said. "I can read the caption under the diagram as well as you can, but I still don't understand what it means or what it does."

"Sorry, I haven't gotten to that page in Mathematics yet," Annie said. "I've been working mostly in other sections. Marcia?"

But it turned out Marcia hadn't gotten to that page in Mathematics yet because she'd been too busy focusing on getting through Language Arts all in one go. None of the rest of us had gotten to that page either.

So we did the sensible thing.

We read what the page had to say about infinity, some of us reading more quickly than others. We waited for those others to finish.

"If I understand correctly," Jackie said, "*infinity* is a word meaning an unlimited extent of time, space, or quantity. So that symbol in relation to numbers is like saying that the number in question is endless. If you could live forever and count forever during that forever life, the number would still be going on."

"Huh," Zinnia said. "It's still a bit confusing, but somewhat less so than before."

Zinnia tilted her head to one side, studying the symbol on the page from a new angle. "Huh," she said again. "When you look at it this way, the infinity symbol looks a bit like an eight lying down."

Seven more heads tilted, plus the heads of the Petes, who'd come in just then to check on us.

We saw that Zinnia was right. An infinity symbol did look like an eight lying down.

"I wonder," Zinnia said, "if we could make our own infinity symbol."

"Could you show us what you have in mind, Zinnia?" Annie said somewhat formally.

How odd for Annie to speak to one of us like that, we thought. And then we realized what Annie was doing: she was trying to let one of us be in charge of something for a change.

"Let's clear a big space in the middle of the floor," Zinnia suggested.

We did that.

"Now let's arrange ourselves," Zinnia said, "like we're one big eight."

"Do you want us to be an infinity symbol or one big eight?" Jackie asked.

Zinnia shrugged. "Both," she said.

"I'm not seeing this," Rebecca said.

We ignored Rebecca although we couldn't see it yet either.

"Annie," Zinnia directed, "lie down on your side and curve your body a little to form one curved end of the eight. Durinda, you hold on to Annie's ankles and curve your hands just slightly. Georgia, you hold on to Durinda's ankles so you can be the line in the center. Jackie, you hold on to Georgia's ankles to continue the line, but curve your legs a bit. Marcia, you grab on to Jackie's curved legs and curve your whole body like Annie's doing to form the other curved end of the eight. Petal, you grab on to Marcia's curved ankles and curve your hands slightly. Rebecca, you hold on to Petal's ankles so you can be the other line in the center, crossing Georgia's line. And now I'll hold on to Rebecca's ankles, and then Annie can grab on to mine when I curve them slightly, like so. There!"

Well, now that we were all in position . . .

"Do you see now?" Zinnia asked excitedly.

"How can I see anything," Rebecca said, "other than Petal's stinky feet. Petal, did you wash these today?"

"Well . . ." Petal said.

The Petes came over and studied the shape we were in on the floor.

"You know," Pete said after a long moment, "I can see it. The eight of you have joined together to form a single eight."

"But if I look at you this way," Mrs. Pete said, tilting her head, "you look like an eight lying down, or an infinity symbol."

"*That's* what I was getting at!" Zinnia said triumphantly.

"Since a few people finally get it," Georgia said, "can we stop doing this now?"

Not waiting for Zinnia's answer, we pulled apart from one another.

"I'm not being critical," Annie said, "but I am curious, Zinnia: what was that about?"

"I don't know." Zinnia shrugged. "Impulse?" she asked as much as answered. "I just suddenly felt as though we should do it, see if we *could* do it. In our world, you never know what might come in handy one day."

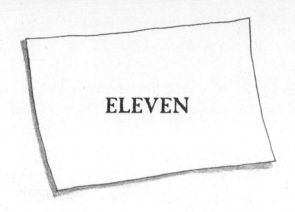

ELEVEN

Being able to turn our eight bodies into one infinity symbol may have felt like a potentially handy thing to know on August 5, but nothing could save us the next day, not when we woke up and realized . . .

It was August 6! Our eighth birthday was just *two days away,* and none of us had done a bit of shopping yet!

"Oh no!" Annie said, being the one to say "Oh no!" for once. Then she proceeded to explain the situation to the Petes.

"With our parents being . . . not around," she concluded after a fair bit of talking, "we'll have no presents for our birthday in two days."

"Of course you'll have presents, pet," Pete said gently.

"We will?" Annie said, shocked.

"Of course you will," Mrs. Pete said. "We have presents for you."

Oh, the Petes were good people.

But . . .

"That truly is wonderful," Annie said, "and we are not ungrateful, but we usually get things for each other as well."

"I don't see why you can't still do that," Pete said. "How do you propose we go about it?"

"Well," Annie said, "the way it usually works is Durinda, Georgia, Jackie, Marcia, Petal, Rebecca, and I go shopping for Zinnia. We go with Mommy while Zinnia stays home with Daddy. Then when we're done with that, Georgia, Jackie, Marcia—"

"I think I see the pattern already," Pete said. "What you're saying is that you go on eight separate shopping trips to get eight separate presents for each other, seven of you going off with your mother while that particular present recipient stays at home with your father."

We were grateful for Pete's quick grasp of the situation, for his immediate understanding of how we did things in our family. If he hadn't understood so fast, we would have waited while Annie listed the eight different casts of characters for the eight separate shopping trips.

We were also grateful, for once, for Annie's ability to take charge of a situation and explain what was required.

"Sure, we can do that," Pete said. "The seven shoppers on each trip will go with Mrs. Pete while I stay here with the particular present recipient."

We did find it odd that he referred to his own wife as Mrs. Pete, but in the face of his generosity we let it go.

"It does sound," Pete added, "as though such an involved shopping process could take all day."

* * * * * * * *

As it turned out, Pete was right.

It *did* take all day, going on eight separate shopping excursions, selecting the perfect present for each particular present recipient, and then getting each present wrapped before returning with it to the cottage.

In fact, we missed the whole day at the beach.

But it was worth it to ensure that at least one part of our birthday would be the same as it always had been in our family.

* * * * * * * *

We awoke the next morning, August 7, to a gorgeous summer day, the kind of day that would be perfect to spend at the beach. But we also awoke to . . .

"Why so glum, chums?" Pete asked.

It was true. We were glum again, depressed.

"I thought," Zinnia said, speaking for all of us, "that it

would be best to be away from home for our eighth birthday — you know, because Mommy and Daddy aren't with us this year. But I'm finding that as tomorrow looms closer, the idea of being away from home on our birthday is even worse, like it's just one change too many in our lives."

"Are you saying you want to go back early?" Pete asked.

"Yes, please," Zinnia said.

We gave her credit for having stellar manners in trying times.

"But we have this cottage for two more days," Mrs. Pete said gently.

"Even still," Zinnia said, "we would like to go today, if you don't mind."

"Of course we don't mind," Pete said.

"Of course we don't," Mrs. Pete said. "We only ever wanted to make you happy."

"So we'll just load up the car," Pete said.

"We won't forget Daddy Sparky and Mommy Sally," Mrs. Pete said.

"Or the *Summer Workbooks*," Annie put in.

"And we'll be on our way," Pete said.

"Well," Mrs. Pete said, "after we drop the keys off with that man at the Little Hotel."

We were going home; we'd make it home in time for our eighth birthday.

We can't say we were cheerful, not at the idea of

spending our first birthday ever without Mommy and Daddy. What a significant birthday to spend without them — the Eights turning eight!

But we were cheered.

* * * * * * *

"Ninety-nine boxes of juice on the wall, ninety-nine boxes of juice!"

Somehow, the trip coming home was never half so fun or exciting as the trip going away.

"I know what we can do to liven things up," Pete said.

He did?

"We could stop at that roadside attraction over there!" Pete suggested enthusiastically when none of us responded.

"What's a roadside attraction?" Petal asked as we piled out of the Hummer.

"It's something on the side of the road," Jackie explained, "almost like a little museum of stuff you'd never get the chance to see at home."

"While you lot look at the roadside attraction," Pete said, "I need to go make a phone call. Back in a tick!"

Huh. We wondered who he'd gone to call so quickly and why he couldn't use the phone in the Hummer.

"So what's this roadside attraction about?" Durinda asked.

"It says that it's a snail farm," Marcia said, reading the little sign.

"My, that looks lively," Rebecca said. "Are any of them even moving?"

* * * * * * * *

"Fifty-three boxes of juice on the wall, fifty-three boxes of juice!"

Wow, we realized. That could get old quickly.

"Time for another roadside attraction," Pete said, "and another phone call."

"Who do you think he's calling?" Marcia wondered.

"And why doesn't he just use our car phone to do it?" Georgia wondered further.

We shrugged.

"What's this roadside attraction for?" Zinnia asked.

"I hope it's not another snail museum." Petal shuddered. "That last one was almost too much excitement for my delicate heart. I nearly fainted."

"Oh, look," Durinda said. "It's a combination museum. On one side, it's a museum of unusual buttons, while on the other, it's a museum of unusual kitchen appliances."

"I'll bet," Rebecca said, "our family could make a better roadside attraction."

* * * * * * * *

All those stops for roadside attractions and one more phone call on Pete's part—as it turned out, the trip back was far longer than the trip out had been.

We arrived back at 6:00 a.m. on August 8, exactly two hours before the official beginning moment of our eighth birthday, 8:00 a.m. being the time Annie was born, with the rest of us being born a minute apart for the next seven minutes.

But that was all okay, because we were home.

Home.

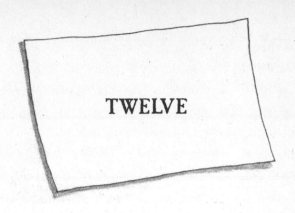

TWELVE

But what was that banner doing draped across our front door? That banner that read — we squinted our eyes against the early-morning light — in tall, rainbow-colored letters...

HAPPY BIRTHDAY, EIGHTS!

It hadn't been there when we left home six days ago. We were almost certain we would have noticed it. Had Carl the talking refrigerator and robot Betty somehow done this? But, we thought, Carl couldn't walk, and Betty's handwriting was never this neat.

"Surprise!" Will Simms shouted, coming around the house from one side.

"Surprise!" Mandy Stenko shouted, coming around the house from the other side.

"Happy birthday, Eights!" the McG and the Mr. McG shouted, coming from wherever such people come from.

"Surprise!" Will and Mandy and the McG and the Mr. McG and the Petes yelled all together.

"You did this," Zinnia said, turning to Pete. "You called them all from the road."

"Well, yes," Pete admitted, "but the missus helped me come up with the idea."

We were relieved he'd stopped calling her Mrs. Pete and was back to calling her the missus.

"Now let's go inside," Pete said, herding us along. "I suspect there are presents and a great big cake waiting for you in there."

* * * * * * * *

The cake waiting for us was big and it was great too; the rainbow lettering on it said *Happy Birthday Annie, Durinda, Georgia, Jackie, Marcia, Petal, Rebecca, Zinnia!*

We were grateful for that cake, the bigness and great-ness of it, and we were doubly grateful that they'd spent the extra money to have all of our names spelled out rather than simply settling for the easier *Happy Birthday, Eights!* Seeing those separate names spelled out like that— it did make each of us feel special.

But we were too excited to open presents and eat cake, too excited from everything that had happened in the past week and everything that was going on. Besides, it wasn't our official birthday yet and wouldn't be until the big clock in the drawing room struck eight.

So instead of opening presents or eating cake, we spent a good bit of time filling in Will and Mandy and the McGs on what we'd been up to on our vacation.

"And then there was no room at the inns," Durinda said, proceeding to tell about that part.

"And then Annie made us do *Summer Workbook*," Georgia said, proceeding to tell about that part.

We could see the McGs were both pleased and im-pressed about that part.

"And then I caught a shadow following me," Petal said, "that everyone thought was my shadow but that turned out to be a boy named George."

"And then," Zinnia said, "actually between some of that and before the rest of it, I called to the dolphins and they came and frolicked with me, with all of us."

Oh, Zinnia.

We stared at her, disappointed in her insistence in keeping on with her fiction, particularly since company had come to call.

She stared back at us, clearly disappointed in our unwillingness to go along with her fiction.

"What?" she said, continuing to stare.

It was odd, how wounded and innocent she looked at that moment.

"Oh, fine," Zinnia said when no one else spoke. "I'm sick of people not believing me, never having faith in me." She paused. "Zither!" she called.

Zither came trotting in.

What was Zinnia doing? we wondered. Was she going to pretend she could talk to one of the cats again?

It was such an old trick; tired, really.

The other cats meandered in, so when Zinnia headed for the front door, Zither by her side, there was a rather large troop of humans and cats trailing behind them.

Where was Zinnia going? we wondered. Was she so angry, angry over our perfectly reasonable and understandable behavior, she was going to run away from home? Or pretend to, like she pretended she could talk to cats and a few other animals?

We watched, rather curiously we will admit, as Zinnia and Zither stepped over the threshold and out a few steps onto the front lawn. In fact, we were so curious, we crowded behind closely, forming an arc around them.

So we were there to see it when Zinnia looked to the sky and nodded slightly. Suddenly there came the sound of thunder, and a greater variety of birds than we'd ever imagined existed filled the whole sky overhead.

Before we could take in what we were seeing, Zinnia leveled her gaze at the street in front of us and then at the woods around us, and she nodded her head again.

And then came all manner of animals imaginable: cats and dogs and bunnies, to be sure, but also larger animals, like lions and tigers and bears and giraffes and kangaroos and pandas and strange animals we didn't even have names for, all of them filling our entire lawn.

We would have been scared, but we were too busy being awed, even Petal.

We were suddenly sure that, if there'd been an ocean nearby, Zinnia could have summoned all the creatures of the sea as well.

"Wow," Georgia whispered in Rebecca's general direction. "When we warned you that you'd better not keep teasing Zinnia about her thinking she could talk to the cats, because who knew what might happen if she really could talk to them, I never imagined it would turn out like this."

Rebecca gulped.

The truth is, none of us had imagined this. None of us *could* have imagined this.

But we should have. We saw that now.

Zinnia was right. We'd never believed what she said, never had faith in her. But we should have. For in the final analysis, what were the options? Zinnia, our sister, had claimed she could communicate with animals. We thought this meant that she was either lying—and we'd never had any other evidence that Zinnia was a liar—or crazy—and we'd never had any other evidence that Zinnia was crazy. That left only one option, really: Zinnia was telling the truth, and she'd been telling the truth all along.

We should have believed her from the start.

We should have had faith.

"Do you believe me now?" she asked quietly without turning around.

We nodded silently. Even though she couldn't see us, we were sure she got the message.

"Does anyone want to check the loose stone in the drawing room?" Zinnia asked, her back still to us.

We shook our heads. We didn't. We knew what any note now would say: that we were a bunch of big fat idiots. Zinnia had had her power all her life, had always known it without needing to be told she had it. It had taken us that long to get wise.

"I'll admit," Zinnia admitted quietly, turning to face us at last, "I always knew I could do . . . *things,* but even I never knew I could do something so large."

Then Zinnia turned, facing forward again, and nodded her head one more time.

All the animals on the lawn parted, creating a path, and one last animal proceeded down that path toward us.

"What is it?" Marcia asked.

"It looks like a horse," Petal said, staring at the snow-white creature, "with a great big horn on its head."

"I don't think it's a horse," Jackie said.

"It's a unicorn," Zinnia informed us in a hushed voice, "the last of its kind in the whole world."

On any other day prior to this one, we might not have believed Zinnia.

But on this day we did.

This really was wonder.

We watched as the unicorn swayed the last few steps to where Zinnia stood, and that's when we noticed the saddle across its back. To the riderless saddle was attached a satchel.

Saddle, satchel — we were tempted to try to say that five times fast but we refrained from doing so.

"Oh," Zinnia said mildly, reaching to take an item sticking out from the satchel, "the unicorn must be here to bring me my gift."

On any other day, we might have doubted her certainty. But not on this one. We might have suggested going to the drawing room to look behind the loose stone so we could see if there was a new note there informing us that Zinnia's gift had arrived, congratulating her, and telling us all in general that there were now sixteen down and zero to go.

But we didn't need to do that. We knew what we were looking at.

We gathered closer around Zinnia to inspect the object she was holding in her hands. The way she held it, turning it this way and that—it was as though it weighed hardly anything at all. The object was a round glass ball sitting on a golden base. Attached to the top of the ball was a tiny circle, and attached to that was a metal hook.

"A Christmas ornament in the shape of a snow globe!" Zinnia said with glee. "I've always loved snow globes!"

It seemed an odd gift for a person to receive: a Christmas ornament in August.

But we didn't think any more of that as we gathered closer still, seeing what Zinnia was seeing: the pretty glass; the stone house within, which despite its miniature size somehow looked practically as big as a mansion but not quite and yet still slightly larger than our own home; the tower room, so similar to ours, jutting out from the top.

Zinnia shook the ornament then, making the glittery dust fly all around the sort-of mansion.

"Wait a second," Zinnia said, peering closer at the ornament. "It looks like there's a person waving his arms, leaning out of the tower window."

Zinnia looked even closer.

We all did.

We *knew* that man, that tiny man who was waving his arms wildly at us.

"*Daddy?*" Zinnia said.